D0205178

CONTEMPORARY AMERICAN FICTION

DESIRES

Award-winning poet, novelist, and short-story writer John L'Heureux taught high school for three years—in Fairfield, Connecticut, and in Boston, Massachusetts. Since then he has taught at Georgetown, Tufts, Harvard, and for the past eighteen years in the English department of Stanford University, where he is Lane Professor of Humanities. L'Heureux has twice been awarded writing fellowships by the National Endowment for the Arts. Four of his earlier works of fiction—*Tight White Collar*, *The Clang Birds*, *Family Affairs*, and *Jessica Fayer*—will be reissued later this year in Penguin editions.

He is married and lives in Palo Alto, California.

DESIRES

JOHN L'HEUREUX

PENGUIN BOOKS

PENGUIN BOOKS
Published by the Penguin Group
Viking Penguin, a division of Penguin Books USA Inc.,
375 Hudson Street, New York, New York 10014, U.S.A.
Penguin Books Ltd, 27 Wrights Lane, London W8 5TZ, England
Penguin Books Australia Ltd, Ringwood, Victoria, Australia
Penguin Books Canada Ltd, 10 Alcorn Avenue, Suite 300,
Toronto, Ontario, Canada M4V 3B2
Penguin Books (N.Z.) Ltd, 182–190 Wairau Road,
Auckland 10, New Zealand

Penguin Books Ltd, Registered Offices:
Harmondsworth, Middlesex, England

First published in the United States of America by Holt, Rinehart and Winston, 1981
Published in Penguin Books 1992

1   3   5   7   9   10   8   6   4   2

PUBLISHER'S NOTE
These stories are works of fiction. Names, characters, places, and incidents either are
the product of the author's imagination or are used fictitiously, and any resemblance to
actual persons, living or dead, events, or locales is entirely coincidental.

Some of the stories in this collection appeared previously in the following publications:
"The Anatomy of Bliss," *The Atlantic*, April 1977. Reprinted in Russian *Amerika*, Moscow,
Spring 1978; "Married Love," *The Ark River Review*, vol. 4, #4, Spring 1980; "The Priest's
Wife," *The Atlantic*, October 1978. Reprinted in *O. Henry Prize Stories*, 1980. Reprinted in
Nineteen: Short Fiction from Stanford, 1980. Reprinted in *Woman's Journal*, London, Autumn
1980; "Consolations of Philosophy," *Esquire*, July 1974; "Brief Lives in California,"
Fiction, vol. 6, #2, Spring 1980; "Departures," *The New Yorker*, April 7, 1980; "Answered Prayers," *Penthouse*, September 1974; "Roman Ordinary," *Harper's*, March 1977;
"Witness," *The Atlantic*, April 1980.

THE LIBRARY OF CONGRESS HAS CATALOGUED THE HARDCOVER AS FOLLOWS:
L'Heureux, John.
Desires.
CONTENTS: Marriages: The anatomy of bliss.
Married love. Love and death in Brighams. The priest's
wife—Mysteries: Consolations of philosophy. Brief
lives in California. Departures. Answered prayers.—
Desires: Roman ordinary. Witness. The anatomy of
desire.
ISBN 0 03 058902 9 (hc.)
ISBN 0 14 01.5223 7 (pbk.)
I. Title.
PS3562.H4D4
813'.54   80–20228

Desires was written partly with the aid of a grant
generously given by the National Endowment for the Arts.

Printed in the United States of America
Designed by Joy Chu

FOR MY WIFE
JOAN POLSTON L'HEUREUX

CONTENTS

The author wishes to thank the editors of the magazines in which some of these stories first appeared: *The Ark River Review, The Atlantic, Esquire, Fiction, Harper's, The New Yorker, Penthouse.*

MARRIAGES

THE ANATOMY OF
BLISS

The problem

The problem, so the shrink says, is whether Calder is willing to put up with his wife's idiosyncrasies. Is he willing? Does he want to? Yes or no.

The problem, as Calder sees it, is the handwriting on the wall.

The wife

The wife's name is Honey-Mae and Calder hates it. Almost any other name is better than Honey-Mae. It sounds trivial. It sounds as if she wears bobbed hair and red circles on her cheeks. As if she speaks with a lisp and sucks pralines all day. Calder hates her name. And she—so Calder tells the shrink—hates him.

The man she hates

Calder. This man is not the hateful sort. He smokes pipes, of course, because he's an academic, and he asks how things are going at the shop, are the orders coming in okay, ahem, and whether or not she remembers to take her One-A-Days. But deep down he is not hateful. No.

He had a vicious streak once, but not anymore. During his childhood he had, with all the other kids, doused a cat with gasoline and then set it on fire. And he had stripped his little sister so that everybody could look. And he did other things.

But when he grew up, he did mostly responsible things and the vicious streak just dried up.

He went to war.

He went to graduate school.

He learned five languages and became a promising assistant professor of comparative literature.

And now he is a dutiful citizen and a loving husband with tenure not far off. So he is, naturally, outraged by the handwriting on the wall.

The child

There isn't any child. Either they can't have one or they haven't hit the right combination yet. Sometimes Honey-Mae mopes around the house and he wonders if that's what it is.

"Is it a child? Is that why you . . . you know?"

"It isn't a child," she says.

"Then what is it? Why do you do it?"

By now it is clear where the scene is going. At the end she says, "I love you," and she cries and this time, again, he does not leave her.

Money

It can't be money, because they have as much as they need.

Work

Honey-Mae never misses a day of work. She chooses material for drapes and sofas and chairs, and her choices are always right. Her clients say there is nobody like Honey-Mae for the perfect decorating touch. So? What is it then?

How it all got started

"What's this?" Calder said.

"What's what?"

"This, under the hook."

Honey-Mae started out of the room.

"It's writing," he said. "It's three words here under the hook."

"I'm taking a bath."

Calder stood outside the bathroom door, suddenly angry. "Honey-Mae," he said, "I'm talking to you. I said what is that writing?"

"I'm taking a bath."

He heard her begin to hum.

Calder had been hanging up his study corduroys on the hook just inside the closet door when he saw what looked like a bug. It was on the wall under the clothes hook and it wasn't moving. He shifted the corduroys to his other hand and gave the bug a quick hard swat. Then he squinted and adjusted his glasses. It wasn't a bug after all. It was handwriting. The writing was very small but the letters were perfectly formed, a little column of three words. He guessed they were words, some kind of words, though they certainly weren't in any of the languages he knew. "What's this?" he had said then to Honey-Mae, but she was having none of it and was sitting in the bath now, humming, while he stood outside the door feeling angry and wondering why.

He went back to the bedroom and finished undressing. He stood before the full-length mirror and looked at himself in profile. He was getting a pot. He sucked in his stomach and watched the bulge disappear. "It's no good," he said to the mirror. "You can't go through life holding your breath." He reached into the closet for his pajamas and threw a quick glance at the corduroy pants. He pushed them tentatively with a finger. The writing was still there. He found himself getting angry again, and feeling foolish too.

Honey-Mae came trailing steam and perfume from the bath and, laughing, she flung herself on top of him.

"Num, num," she said.

"Listen," he said, "what's that writing in the closet?"

"I don't know about any writing," she said, her decorator's hands busy with his pajama tops. "I'll make little patterns on your chest," she said.

He made a mental note to show her the writing in the closet, afterward, but Honey-Mae was playing tiger lady right now, and what the hell.

"You're so good," she said, her voice gone velvet.

"Mmmm," he said.

The next day the writing was still there. He shrugged and made another mental note to ask her about it and then forgot.

A week later there was a fourth word and then a fifth. He was sure there had been only three. Honey-Mae was getting her robe from the closet just then, and he took her arm and turned her, saying, "Lookit. What's this?"

And that was how it all got started.

The writing

The writing is small, in a cursive hand, made by a blue ball-point pen, fine-tipped. The words are of varying length, but they spell nothing.

Calder has copied out the words in his most careful hand. He has consulted his dictionaries and his texts on dialectic and grammar. He has even consulted the awful T. D. Wood, who knows everything. But the words spell nothing.

It must be a code of some kind. Calder is at work studying books on code when suddenly two more words appear. This is it. This calls for scrupulous scientific analysis. While Honey-Mae is at the shop, he sets up special lights and he photographs the words exactly as they appear beneath the hook in his closet. He has the prints blown up to five times their size. He compares; he isolates; he grinds his teeth in frustration. He feeds the words into a computer—forwards, then backwards, then any old way. It is hopeless. It isn't a code. Or perhaps the code is incomplete.

Calder has begun gaining weight. He eats absent-mindedly, but all the time, and he has begun dreaming that threats are being made on his life. But all the threats are in code. He tells Honey-Mae none of this. He is determined she must not know, though he can't say why. But who can be writing these words? Who is doing it?

The problem

"Well, if you're not doing it, who is? Somebody's doing it."

"Why are you so angry?" Her reasonable voice. "It's only a little writing on the closet wall. Nobody's ever even going to see it."

"Maybe it's Amber. It must be Amber."

"Get dressed, Calder. You're going to be late."

"But why would Amber want to write on the closet wall?"

Amber

Amber has cleaned house in this neighborhood for the past fifteen years. During that time professors or their wives have accused her of hitting the dog, spoiling the children, drinking the liquor, smoking the grass (Professor Wood, the accuser), and sitting down on the job. She has never been accused of writing on the wall. She quits.

The man she loves

There are ten words now. Now there are fifteen. Now twenty. Calder has no control over it. He wishes they were not there. He wills them not to be there. But there they are, tiny irregular scratches descending in a perfect row beneath the hook in the closet. Words. In no language he knows. He says nothing more about it to Honey-Mae. They pretend to each other that the words are not there.

But now they have made love, and it is good, and they are lying against one another, counting breaths. He kisses her wet forehead. She sighs and nuzzles him. And then he says it.

"It is you, isn't it. Making those marks."

"Marks?"

"Marks. On the wall. In the closet."

"No."

"It is."

"No, Calder. I swear it isn't."

They lie together, silent. Honey-Mae moves her shoulder against him, but he does not respond.

"You do believe me, don't you? Calder?"

"Yes. I want to. Yes, I do."

"I love you," she says.

In the morning he is full of energy and when she comes out of the bathroom, brisk, ready for work, he mentions almost casually, "You know, it's the damnedest thing. Where do you suppose those words are coming from?"

And just as casually, she says, "I wrote them."

Calder stares at her, a pain in his chest. "You? But you told me . . ."

"Oh, for God's sake, Calder, don't make such a big thing out of everything." And then she is off to work.

The shop

Mrs. Fischer is leafing through a book of sample brocades. Each time she turns a heavy page, she fingers it, and checks Honey-Mae's reaction. The tiniest frown, the tilt of the head in a question, the pursed lip. Mrs. Fischer has not yet made the right choice.

Honey-Mae is sitting at her little antique desk helping Mrs. Fischer select the fabric for a Queen Anne wing chair. Honey-Mae wears her oyster pants suit with the beige silk blouse. She is short and shouldn't be able to get away with a pants suit, but somehow she does. Her blond hair, clipped close to her head, emphasizes her delicate features. She uses no makeup except a gray pencil above her lashes. Her eyes are large and gray. Sitting there, expectant, encouraging, she is herself the most impressive sample of her art.

Honey-Mae smiles gently as Mrs. Fischer touches for a second time the melon and gold brocade that is perfect for her wing chair.

"This one, I think," Mrs. Fischer says.

"Perfect," Honey-Mae says.

Perfection. The brocade is perfect, and so is the shop, and so is Honey-Mae. Yet, in less than a quarter-hour Honey-Mae is on the telephone to Calder, sobbing over and over "Forgive me, forgive me."

Celebration

Calder has been voted tenure and so they are going to dinner at The Silly Goose to celebrate. "Life is good sometimes," Calder says. He reaches into the closet for his dark blue suit and checks the wall beneath the coat hook. Smooth, white, unspotted. He shouldn't have checked it, but he can't help himself. After their last fight Honey-Mae had scrubbed the wall with Bon Ami and most of the writing had come out. Later he thought he saw signs that new words had been written and then erased, but he was never sure. Anyway, no words are there now, and he shouldn't be checking.

The celebration is perfect. A tenderloin of lamb and a Nuits Saint Georges and, before bed, there will be some very good brandy. And the two of them together, in love, with no writing on the wall.

She is in the bath now and Calder carries the little silver tray with the two snifters into the bedroom and puts it on her bureau. Perfect.

Suddenly he thinks how he can surprise her. He goes to her side of the closet and looks for the lace negligee he bought her on their honeymoon in Florence. White chiffon. Where is it? His fingers flick through her dresses, but there is no negligee. Just as he decides that it must be in the bureau, his eye catches the long skirt through a transparent plastic cover, way in the back, against the wall. He takes it out carefully, making sure it does not catch on anything. And then he gasps, holding the gown crumpled against him. He stares straight ahead at the wall, the white wall, covered from top to bottom in minute handwriting, words, words in long columns, in perfect lines. Words covering the entire wall.

Honey-Mae is standing behind him, naked and perfumed. She looks at him with disgust, with hatred. She turns and walks, wooden, to the bed.

Calder takes the brandy to his study. He sits in his big leather chair, gazing helplessly at the books everywhere around him. He drinks the brandy, and keeps on drinking until he is drunk.

The problem

"Why?" he says. He is begging her. "Please. Just tell me. I want to understand. Why do you do it?"

"What does it matter?" Honey-Mae says, surly, not herself. "You've never loved me anyway."

The lovers

Calder and Honey-Mae have decided on a frank talk. The morning light streams through the blinds and a frank talk seems the sensible way to begin the day, to begin a new life.

"I just want you to be happy," Calder says.

"I know. I know that." Honey-Mae burrows into his chest.

"No, I don't want you to burrow now. I want us to have a frank talk. Will you do that for me?"

Honey-Mae sits up, all business.

"I just want you to be happy," he starts again.

"I know that."

"And if you're writing on the walls like this, something must be the matter."

She says nothing.

"Right?"

"I'm not writing on the walls."

He says nothing.

"Suppose I did?" she says suddenly. "Suppose I threw shit all over the walls? So what? You've done worse."

"Me! I! What have I ever done?"

"Well, I'm not writing on the walls."

"This is hopeless. There's no sense trying to have a frank talk with you. Nothing ever follows in logical order. There's never any sequence. It's just denial and accusation. I thought we were friends. I thought we loved one another." He says the last part bitterly and pushes his way out of bed.

"Calder?" Honey-Mae tugs at his sleeve as he sits at the edge of the bed fishing for his slippers. "Calder, I'm sorry. I'll try. I'm trying my best."

Honey-Mae hides her face in the pillow and begins to cry. Calder bends over her, smoothing her shoulders and back. He kisses the nape of her neck, slowly, lovingly. She turns and pulls him down on top of her.

And then he asks, "But what are you writing? Or what do you *think* you're writing?"

"I just do it," she says, her face turned away now.

"But why? Words have to mean something. Why?"

"Why can't you *be* with me?"

"But I *am* with you."

They are silent for a while: he staring at her profile, she with her face to the wall. Finally she speaks, her voice shattered.

"You understand nothing," she says. "Nothing."

The shrink

Dr. Robertson practices at the University Medical Health Center but he takes some private patients too. The problems are always the same, variations on a theme.

"She writes on the walls?" he says, with only half a smile.

"The closet walls, only."

"Do you know why she does this?"

"No. That's the problem. That's why I'm here."

"And how do you feel about it?"

Calder gives a very long, very clear explanation of how

he feels about Honey-Mae's writing on the walls and when he finishes, Dr. Robertson is silent.

"The *Goldberg Variations,*" Dr. Robertson says finally.

"Pardon me?"

"Or *The Art of Fugue.*"

"Bach?" Calder says.

"Tell me about you. Tell me what you want out of life."

Surprise

In class Calder lectures on the mythic elements common to Don Juan, Don Quixote, and Faust. He is happy. He forgets what awaits him at home. As he crosses the campus to his car, however, the tension begins and by the time he reaches home, he is covered in sweat. How can this be happening? Is he losing his mind? He pauses at the front door and pretends to examine the lawn. Everybody in this town is crazy on the subject of crabgrass, so nobody is going to care if he stands there for an hour staring at the ground. Finally, sick, he puts his key in the door and goes inside.

"Honey-Mae?" There is no answer. "Honey-Mae?" he calls again, a new sound in his voice.

Honey-Mae is working only half-time these days and if she does not answer, it means only one thing. Calder squares his shoulders and walks down the corridor into the sunlit bedroom. Honey-Mae is lying unconscious on the bed, but Calder only glances at her as he strides across the room. The closet door is open and the floor is heaped with clothes.

The walls are covered with writing.

That month

For one whole month everything has been perfect. Honey-Mae has painted the closet and she has not gone near a pencil. Calder brings her flowers every other day, they dine out on the weekends, they are friends.

"What do you suppose it was?" he asks her.

That look comes over Honey-Mae's face and, as it does, he feels something tighten in his chest.

"I mean, do you think it was tension, or overwork, or something? Maybe you were worried for me, that I wouldn't get tenure. I mean, it has to have some logical explanation."

"Why do you have to bring it up?" she says. "Do you *like* to humiliate me? Don't you think I'm disgraced enough?"

"You?" he says. "You! That makes me laugh. What about me? Do you have any idea what it's like to live with a crazy woman? Do you have any idea what it's like to be at school, talking about Don Juan and the perfection of unattainable ideals, and be thinking Yes, by now she's finished one wall and is moving on to the next one? She wants to have the whole closet finished by the time I get home. For a surprise. For a treat. And meanwhile the kids are looking at one another, figuring I'm losing my mind. Christ, it's out of *Jane Eyre*, the loony in the attic. You make me sick. You disgust me. I wish to God I'd never laid eyes on you."

Later, much later, he wakes her up and says he is sorry.

"I've got a vicious streak in me, I guess."

"It's my fault."

"It's mine too."

"Will you hold me?" she says.

She is shivering and when he takes her in his arms, she clutches at him, pressing her body into his.

"Make love to me, please. Please."

And he does, frightened, because he is making love to a stranger.

The handwriting on the wall

Honey-Mae is writing on the walls every day now and she makes no secret of it. She goes to the shop in the morning where she sees customers and puts in orders for fabric and furniture and accessories. She does her work well. By noon she is back at home and she writes without stopping until she collapses or until she hears Calder at the front door. He comes in and stares at the writing and stares at her. Sometimes he tells her he loathes her. Sometimes he tells her she needs help. But mostly he tells her that unless she stops and stops now, he will leave her. She says nothing. She turns to the wall, covered with her tiny script, and she sleeps.

The problem

Calder stops suddenly in the middle of his lecture comparing the poetic vision of Saint John of the Cross with the mystic vision of Cervantes. It has just struck him that he has no idea what he is talking about. After a minute he goes on anyway.

The problem

Honey-Mae wakes him in the middle of the night and says, "I love you, Calder. You are the only one. I love you. I love you."

Calder lies there with his eyes closed, his hand dutifully caressing her back.

Data

"I've had it. I'm done with her. I want out."

Dr. Robertson raises his eyebrows one-sixteenth of an inch.

"I know how that sounds, but I want out."

"Well, that's a choice you have to make."

"I don't *want* to leave her, but I've got to. I can't take any more. I'm not sleeping, my work is going to pot, I look like hell. *She* looks like hell too, for that matter. I've done everything I can think of. I've begged her to stop. I've pleaded. I've tried to be understanding. I've been a bastard, too, I can't help it. I've got this vicious streak and she brings it out in me. You should see the walls. It's unbelievable. It's a crazy house. It is! The bedroom, the bathroom, the kitchen. She's even started now on the living room. She's left my study alone, that's the only place. I go in there and get drunk."

"She's left your study alone."

"Oh, she'd never write in there."

"Why is that?"

"She just wouldn't. It's where I, you know, *do* everything. My writing, my books. She wouldn't."

"And you get drunk there."

"Well, only sometimes."

"And why do you get drunk?"

"To escape. You know, just to get away from it."

"And do you?"

Calder looks at the shrink. Forty dollars an hour for this.

"I come back to the study," Dr. Robertson says. "Why do you suppose she leaves that, of all the other rooms, untouched? What do you suppose it represents to her?"

"It's where I work. It's . . . oh God . . . it's . . ."

"It's where you go to escape, you said. It's where you *do* everything, you said. Your writing, your books."

"Yes?"

"That's what you said."

"Yes."

"Is she trying to tell you something? This Honey-Mae? Is she trying to make you notice her? And even while she's doing it, protecting your most secret place? What if she should invade that place? What would that mean to you?"

"She wouldn't."

"But if she did?" The shrink is wearing his little half-smile.

"She wouldn't."

"She may." Pause. Tick tick tick. "She will."

"I love her. She's crazy, but I love her."

"You have to decide what you want," the shrink says.

"What I want."

"And then get it."

The woman he loves

Honey-Mae has put on the weight she lost and she is back at work.

She has painted the walls of every room except Calder's study. She never goes in there.

She does not write on the walls.

She is the perfect wife.

The woman he hates

Honey-Mae has done it again. But only a little bit. In the bedroom closet.

Calder flings his glass across the room, almost at her but not quite, and then he slams out of the house. In a minute he is back, with a purpose.

He goes to his study and comes back with a marking pen. In huge black script he writes I HATE YOU across the bedroom wall. He writes it three more times and then he turns to face her. She is slumped against the door, her head bowed. Her small body shakes as she cries silently.

The shrink

Honey-Mae has agreed to see Dr. Robertson. Calder waits in the reception room until she comes out, pale, smiling faintly.

"What did he say?" Calder asks as soon as they are in the car.

"He says I am unhappy."

"But why do you write? Did he say? Does he know?"

"He said it sounds to him that I do it because I'm unhappy."

"Forty bucks for that?"

"I'm sorry." She covers her face with her hands.

"What's the use," he says. "What's the use of anything."

Resolutions

Calder is listening to a student talk about the subtle connection between Saint Teresa's *Interior Castle* and Franz Kafka's *The Castle* when Calder suddenly realizes something and blurts out, "She is unhappy."

"What?"

"Can we talk tomorrow?" Calder is all action now, gathering books, throwing papers into his satchel. "Let's talk tomorrow. I have to get home."

"Who's unhappy?" the student says.

"I have to go."

Calder tosses the satchel into a corner and makes a break for the door, leaving the student behind. "Unhappy," he says. He knows what he will find when he gets home, but it doesn't matter.

He runs a yellow light at Fifth and Bryant and another one at the corner of his own street, but he knows he won't get caught. Not now. Not today. "She is unhappy," he says aloud, to nobody. "Unhappy." His heart races because it may be too late. He bounds up the walk, into the house, straight to his study.

Honey-Mae is on her knees, so engrossed in her work that she does not even turn at the sound of his steps.

Beside her and behind her rise long shelves of books, some with torn jackets, some with notepaper sticking out of them. She has pushed aside the heavy desk, loaded with his papers, notes for lectures, outlines for articles he will write.

She kneels before the wall, which had been white this morning, and which now is covered with words. But not columns of words this time, not random scratchings. No, the words grow from the baseboard and rise up the long length of white wall into airy patterns of trees and flowers and animals. The words are all in different colors, written close together, so that you do not see happy unhappy happy, you see only the flowering tree the words have formed, and on the tip of the longest thinnest branch the delicate shining blossom that says bliss, over and over.

Honey-Mae kneels before her work, before this blessed jungle, creating words, oblivious.

"It's all right," he says.

At the sound of his voice she crouches and hides her face. He has never actually seen her writing before. He kneels beside her, carefully, and strokes her hair.

"It's all right," he says very softly. "I know. I know."

She lifts her face to him and he kisses her, first on the brow and then, almost formally, on the lips.

"I understand," he says again. She turns to face him and he watches, astounded, as slowly slowly the madness drains from her eyes.

They sink to the floor and lie there in each other's arms, not making love, only looking. Above them are his books and his papers and the flowers and trees full of happiness, unhappiness, happiness they have finally made.

But he and she do not look at the wall; they lie next to it and stare into each other; looking, and looking.

MARRIED LOVE

In love

In love, nothing is merely itself. The flowers that arrive unexpectedly, the light touch across the restaurant table, the knowing smile: these can be a promise or a reminder or a murder threat. Everything is something else, in love.

Mrs. Woodbridge

Mrs. Woodbridge cast an anxious look at the ringing telephone. She was in love, and she was contemplating the object of her love, and so the ringing telephone caused her only minor anxiety. She looked back to the television set where lively things were happening on a rerun of "The Gong Show." A very old lady wearing roller skates and a tutu was playing "Moonlight Sonata" on the violin. Her hair was dyed yellow and piled high in a nest of many curls, and her face was thick with layers of makeup, so she was not an object of pity. Objects of pity looked pathetic, they were a mess. Not this lady. She was just an old tart having a good time on roller skates. Nonetheless Rex Reed gave her the gong.

"You look so cute there in your little outfit," Chuck Barris, the host, said to the lady on roller skates. He gave her a nice little hug and then he asked Rex Reed, "Why did you do that, Rex?"

"Because," Rex Reed said, "in the immortal words of Gore Vidal, 'Merely not having talent is no longer enough.' "

Everyone in the audience laughed at that, even though it was hard to understand, and then there was an advertisement for Blistex. Mrs. Woodbridge was interested in Chuck Barris, not in Blistex, and so she answered the phone, which was still ringing.

"Hello," she said, a woman in love, but it was her husband calling to let her know that he was sending a man over for an estimate on the chimney. "Not now," she said. "Not during my show." But the chimney man showed up right away, while "The Gong Show" was still on. "You'll have to wait," she said to him and he sat with her on the white couch until "The Gong Show" was over.

"What is this anyhow?" the man said. "How can you watch that stuff?"

"It is my favorite show," she said.

"But they're all loonies. They're all crazy people. It's not even nice to laugh at those people."

"I like Chuck Barris," she said, and added quickly, to throw him off, "and the midget at the end. I like it when the midget throws confetti at everybody."

"Well, it beats me," the man said. "Let's take a look at that chimney."

He lay down on his back and angled his head up the chimney and made tsk-ing noises.

"What is the matter with the chimney?" she said.

"Let me look at the boiler," he said. "I have to check it all out."

She led him down the steep steps to the cellar. He smiled when he saw the boiler.

"What?" she said.

"It's been a long time since I've seen one of these," he said. "This is a real old-timer." He looked into the boiler and made more tsk-ing noises. Then he looked at Mrs. Woodbridge and said, "Basically what you need is a whole new furnace setup, but if you watched 'Sixty Minutes' last week you know that we now have a device I can attach that will cut your heat bills by thirty-three percent, more or less. Three hundred bucks."

"Three hundred?"

"Can you swing that? What does your husband do?"

"Mr. Woodbridge is in shirts."

"Oh."

They were silent for a long while and then the chimney man said, "You have very big boobs. They are very attractive, if you get me, but there is no denying they are very big."

"You should not talk to me that way," she said. "I am a married woman."

"Ah, come on," he said, nudging her. "I bet you have a lover," he said, "what with those big boobs and all."

"Well, sort of," she said, and then he did many interesting things with her boobs and she let him. When he left the house she asked herself, "Will this be the only time?" And she answered herself, "I should never have told him Mr. Woodbridge is in shirts."

Her husband

Her husband was in shirts. In the old days he had gone around with a large case filled with shirts and showed them to managers of department stores, but then IBM and ITT and Crowell-Collier Communications Industries took over all the department stores and brought in their own shirt suppliers, and so Mr. Woodbridge had to discover a new place to push shirts. He discovered boutiques. The firm he represented was very pleased with what he was doing in boutiques, and they paid him enough money to live on, but not enough for him to lay out three hundred for an attachment to his boiler. He was disheartened when Mrs. Woodbridge told him what the chimney man had said.

"God dammit," he said, "we can't afford three hundred for the boiler."

"That's in addition to three hundred to clean the chimney," she said.

"We'll do the chimney," he said, "but not the boiler."

"I hope they send a different man for the chimney," she said.

"What the hell is this stuff we're eating?" he said.

"Tripe," she said.

"What a life," he said.

Her lover

Her lover was a married man, for all she knew. But that didn't stop her. No. Passion must have its head. She wrote him letters each day and bought many movie magazines in hope of finding his photograph. At night she dreamed of him. He did not write back to her and she did not know what he dreamed about. But that did not matter. She was in love with Chuck Barris, host of "The Gong Show," host of her most indelicate fantasies. She loved her husband too, of course.

The chimney

The chimney was an ordinary brick chimney that maybe had an accumulation of soot. Whatever the reason, Mr. Woodbridge could see it wasn't drawing properly. The one comfort he had in life was a cozy fire in the fireplace after a long day's hoofing around the boutiques.

"We've got to have that damned chimney fixed," he said. He had lit another fire, because maybe after all the chimney man was wrong, but it turned out he wasn't wrong and now, again, the living room was filled with smoke. "What do I get out of life? I'd like to know. I shag ass around shopping malls day in, day out, I come home dropping, is a fire too much to ask? I ask you. In my own fireplace? We've got the estimate, let's have the damned thing fixed."

Mr. Woodbridge was right; they had the estimate on the chimney—three hundred clammerinos—but for a full week the chimney man did not show up. Then, Monday, at exactly 1:15, the doorbell rang and who was there but him.

"Ta-daaaa!" he said, pointing to Mrs. Woodbridge's boobs and rolling his eyes obscenely.

"Not now," she said. "I'm in the middle of my show."

So he sat down beside her on the white couch and waited. It seemed the show would take forever because there was a man who put his hands over his face and made poop noises to the tune of "Home on the Range." Then there were two girls who wore a cow costume and tap-danced.

"The back of the cow is out of sync with the front part," the chimney man said.

"Shhhh!" Mrs. Woodbridge said. "Never mind the cow. Chuck will be on in a second."

"Who's Chuck? What's this Chuck?"

Rex Reed gonged the cow and everybody applauded and, sure enough, Chuck Barris came from behind the curtain, rubbing his hands and smiling. "I thought you were great," he said, squeezing the arm of the girl who was the front of the cow. "You're so nice and fresh and scrubbed. You're so cute."

"Oh, I just adore him," Mrs. Woodbridge said, blowing kisses to the television set. "I love you, I love you," she said.

The chimney man was put out by her excitement and just sat back for a while and said nothing.

Finally the winner was announced, a girl who had done a very nice belly dance. The midget pelted her with confetti and pretty soon it was all over.

The chimney man just sat there sulking. "He's the one? This Chuck?" he said. "He's your sort-of lover?"

"He's wonderful," she said. "He sees the good in everyone."

"What's so special about that? I see the good in everyone. I saw the good in you, right away, didn't I? So what's he got that I haven't got?"

"He's my whole life to me. And besides, what do I know about you? You're practically a stranger," Mrs. Woodbridge said.

The chimney man could see she was serious and he was deeply offended. "Well, you can *touch* me; you can't *touch* him."

"I wouldn't want to touch him. I don't love him in that way."

"Well, put it another way. *He* can't touch you and I *can*. He's up there on the screen. Right?"

There was a long silence.

"You'd better fix the chimney," she said.

Without another word he went out to his truck and got the thirty-gallon canister and the suction equipment and went about the messy business of cleaning the chimney. Mrs. Woodbridge hovered around, but he ignored her.

In midafternoon Mr. Woodbridge telephoned to say that the chimney people were sending a man out today and Mrs. Woodbridge told him the man was already here. "Thank God," he said, "for small favors." She went back and told the chimney man that her husband had called and she told him what he said.

"Sure, he's out selling shirts, wearing a nice suit and tie, buying lunch and drinks for store managers—"

"Boutique managers."

"—boutiques, whatever, padding the old expense account. And me? I'm up to my krogies in soot, cleaning out his filthy chimney. And he says thank God for small favors. That's rich! That's what you call irony!"

She went away and made tea then, Darjeeling, and in a while she brought him a cup. They drank tea squatting by the boiler.

"I never meant it to be this way," she said.

"It could have been so different," he said.

So they took a shower together and, though he refused to fool around with her boobs, for a while everything was different. It was like old times, so she gave him a half-dozen of her husband's best white-on-white shirts.

On the way out the chimney man patted the fireplace bricks and said, "You can tell your husband he's got the cleanest chimney on the block. I stand by my work."

That night

That night Mr. Woodbridge started a fire in the fireplace and, just as it had before, the smoke poured out into the living room. He and Mrs. Woodbridge ran for pots of water and put the fire out, but it was a long time before they got rid of the smoke.

"I'll call the chimney people tomorrow," Mr. Woodbridge said, near tears. "All I ask is to be able to start a fire in my fireplace. Is that unreasonable? Is that asking too much?"

The next day

The next day at the home office Mr. Woodbridge talked over his problem with Harry. Harry said, "Cripes, Woodbridge, you've been taken. What you do is call the Better Business Bureau. You call the bank and stop that check. You call the attorney general's office. What's the matter with you anyhow? You've been in shirts too long."

Mr. Woodbridge called all these people and he tried to stop payment on his check, but it was too late. When there was nobody left to call, he called the chimney people themselves. They assured him that this had never happened before. They assured him if he tried to stop his check, they'd make trouble with his credit rating. They assured him he wouldn't have a prayer in a lawsuit. Meanwhile they would send somebody over soon to see what was amiss with his chimney.

Smack in the middle of "The Gong Show," the doorbell rang.

"Ta-daaaa!" he said, but again Mrs. Woodbridge made him wait.

Toward the end of the show Chuck Barris took off his big bow tie and said, "Stay tuned. In a moment we'll be back with more STUFF."

"It's the way he says 'stuff,' " she said.

"I'll show you stuff," the chimney man said, and pulled her toward him on the white couch. She kicked and scratched and they tumbled onto the floor, and he felled her finally with a smack from his elbow, but he did not let her go back to watching "The Gong Show." From her position on the floor she could hear the music they always played when the midget pelted everybody with confetti, but he would not even let her look. "I've had enough of this nonsense," he said. "What kind of woman has a love affair with a television screen? You are an unwell person. I could have you committed."

They made up, tenderly, and for old times' sake he did some of his interesting things with her boobs.

Before he left, she gave him some more of her husband's shirts. Then he went down to the cellar and checked all the flues and everything looked pretty good.

"Tell your husband the smoke is all in his head," he said.

Mr. Woodbridge

Mr. Woodbridge had put in a tough day at the boutiques and all he wanted now was a nice fire and no crap to deal with. He took a shower and changed his clothes. He couldn't help noticing the big difference in his shirt drawer. He shook his head, shed a tear or two, and then shrugged. There was no point in calling the attorney general; nobody wanted any trouble.

Downstairs again, he lit a couple of sheets of newspaper in the fireplace to make sure it was drawing properly. Everything looked okay.

"How was your day?" Mrs. Woodbridge said as they stood watching the flames from the newspaper.

"It's good to be home," he said.

He lit two more sheets and they burned all right, though there was some smoke. "Is it smoky in here?" he said.

"Maybe we have to expect a little smoke at the beginning," she said.

So he lit a good big fire and almost at once the smoke poured into the living room and Mr. Woodbridge began to yell dirty words and then he ran for pots of water.

Much later, when she had fed him soup and crackers

and held his head in her lap on the white couch, he said, "Well, what's done is done. All the same, I'm going to find out what the hell's going on up there." He lay on his back and angled his head up into the chimney and immediately noticed that the hook on the lever that pushes open the flue had come loose. He slipped the hook back in place and tested it. It held. He pushed the flue open and shut several times. "It's fixed," he said. "The problem was that the flue wasn't open, that's all."

"We paid three hundred dollars for that?" Mrs. Woodbridge said. "Not to mention the inconvenience."

Mr. Woodbridge was very pale. "Let's just enjoy our fire," he said.

"The Gong Show"

"The Gong Show" was wonderful all that week. There were dancers and singers and a lady in a red dress with boobs even bigger than Mrs. Woodbridge's who both sang and danced. When that particular lady finished her performance, the phone rang and it was the chimney man.

"Did you see that?" he said. "What do you make of that?"

"I've got to go," she said. "Chuck is going to be on straightaway."

"Never mind this Chuck," he said. "I could come over there and ring the old gong myself. Huh? Huh?

"What are you, crazy?" he said, when he heard the receiver click. "Nobody hangs up on me. We've got something going here, something really beautiful. You can't do this to me after what we've shared together. You hear? You hear?" But of course she didn't hear because she had hung up. "I'll get you," he said.

Jealousy

Jealousy is one of the tricky emotions. Who is it who is being loved? The lover? The loved one? Or that third party? Everything is something else, in love.

Revenge

Revenge was the only thing in the chimney man's mind when he showed up the next day wearing one of Mr. Woodbridge's white-on-white shirts. Mrs. Woodbridge was watching "The Gong Show" and she ignored him while he trundled in and out of the house with armfuls of bricks and then a bag of cement and a small mixing trough. When the show was over, she said to him, "What are you doing in that white-on-white shirt and what is all this stuff?"

"I've had enough of Chuck Barris," he said. "I'm going to end your affair once and for all."

He dragged the heavy television set from its niche in the wall and set it up inside the fireplace. Mrs. Woodbridge protested and beat him about the back and shoulders, but he kept right on. Methodically he lay row upon row of bricks across the fireplace opening. Layer by layer, the television screen disappeared. Very near the end he tore off the white-on-white shirt and stuffed it through the opening. Then he cemented in the final row of bricks. He tidied the place. He dragged out the extra mortar, he removed his drop cloth, he swept away the tiny fragments of brick and cement. And then he stood there, hands on hips, next to the solid wall of bricks.

"Well," he said. "This is how you wanted it. Now you've got what you want." He shook his head sadly.

"I never wanted it to turn out this way," she said.

"You and that fool on television," he said.

"You're the fool," she said. "Do you think for a second that I can't get a new television set? And to think I ever gave you those white-on-white shirts!"

"Castoffs!" he said. "I should have known then. What a fool I've been to waste my time on you."

And then he flung out of the house so that he would have the last word in the end.

The end

The end was worse than she had feared. That night Mr. Woodbridge came bouncing in, rubbing his hands and saying, "Let's have a fire." At once he spied the solid wall of bricks. For a long time he simply stood there staring at what used to be his fireplace and then, slowly, in pain, he sat down on the edge of the white couch and let his head fall into his hands. The clock on the mantel ticked loudly in the silent room.

Finally, sobbing, he said to Mrs. Woodbridge, "Why? Why?"

"I know," she said, sobbing too. "I know. I know."

LOVE AND DEATH IN BRIGHAMS

1
. . .

The old lady in Brighams has ordered a cup of coffee and a chocolate milk shake but she's not paying a great deal of attention to either of them. She has her eye on the young man and the young woman in the booth next to her. From where she is sitting she can see right into his coffee cup; if she wanted to, she could nudge the young woman and say, "Pass the sugar" or something. She is that close.

The young man and the young woman are trying to engage in normal conversation even under the gaze of the old lady. She relents for a minute—she looks beyond them at the mirrored wall where she can watch them in reverse— and at once the young man pounces.

"That old lady has a cup of coffee *and* a milk shake," he says, with italics.

"Don't stare."

The old lady returns her gaze to him, straight on.

"The trouble with Brighams," he says in a public voice, "is their coffee is never hot."

"Ask for some more," the old lady says across the booth divider. And as the two young people look over at her, she adds, "Sure. The old bottomless cup. Ask for some more."

2
. . .

In a story the narrator would tell us that the young man and the young woman are actually forty-two years old, that they are not very happily married, that they have come to Brighams this Saturday morning as a blind act of faith. Maybe (so the narrator would explain) if she spends an hour shopping for wineglasses (give them a party that night) while he has a good hour at the library (make him an amateur historian, or botanist, or bibliophile), then maybe they could meet for lunch at Brighams and everything would seem normal to them. He would forget that in his notebook he has three times this week recorded his intention to kill himself. She would forget that she has gone down on her knees and prayed the rosary (make her Catholic, make her a former nun. No, that's been done. A nurse?) daily for a month asking God to keep her from plunging a knife into his skinny (hairy?) chest. Going to Brighams this day is an act of faith in the power to forget. To be normal. To be a smiling couple having a sandwich and a cup of coffee, in Brighams.

3
. . .

Problems about starting with the old lady

1. Takes the focus off the young people. Young? You've made them forty-two. That's a further problem. Nobody cares about people who are still messing up their lives at age forty-two.

2. People care even less about old ladies (make her somewhere in her sixties, maybe even younger) who are still messed up after a whole lifetime in which to straighten things out. People like feisty old ladies or eccentric old ladies, especially rich ones, but not old ladies per se.

3. Merely ordering a cup of coffee and a chocolate milk shake is not enough to catch the reader's attention. Now, take the case of the man in yesterday's paper who was arrested for spreading rat poison on crackers and eating them. In Howard Johnson's. Something like that would catch the reader's attention and hold it.

4. Giving her rat poison, on the other hand, makes her merely crazy and craziness of itself is not interesting. Craziness has no rules. A story, a character, has to have rules; at least its own rules.

5. How can the young people (aged forty-two!) and this old lady interact in a way that will produce a story?

Proposed solutions

1. Forget the old lady. Or, if her story stands up to the test of time (if the narrator can't get it out of his head a year from now), then put her in another story, her own.

2. Forget the young people. They present difficulties of an even more pressing kind: either he's got to go off and kill himself or she's got to plunge that knife deep into his hairy (skinny?) chest.

3. Forget the whole thing.

4
· · ·

"Ask for some more," the old lady says across the booth divider. "Sure. The old bottomless cup. Ask for some more."

And so he does. And in time the waitress (make her sixteen, glad to have this part-time job at minimum wage, unaware it is her right to be rude to anybody who asks for more coffee, for more anything), all smiles and blushes, brings more coffee. The young man smiles at her and at the young woman and then takes a sip. He has been ignoring the old lady.

"Hot?" the young woman says.

"How's that?" the old lady says. "Is it hot enough for you? If it isn't, ask for some more."

"It's fine," he says.

"They're always good about that here," the old lady says. "I come here every day of my life. There's never any problem with the food. It's not the Ritz, you understand, but it's okay."

"Yes," he says. He is determined to salvage their morning, their act of faith. He looks hard at the young woman and, because she returns his look, they agree to turn the old lady off. Sayonara, old lady. He leans forward and says softly, to show this is a private conversation, "I must write to Mike Rubin and tell him the kind of winter I got myself in for."

"He'll be amused," the young woman says, "knowing how you hate the cold."

"Isn't this something? This cold?" the old lady says, turned off but still talking. "We haven't had a winter like this since . . . well, when?"

(Make it January, make it New England, the worst winter in recorded history. Evidently the young man is not from New England. This Mike Rubin he is going to write is somebody who is well away from the cold.)

"How do you think it will be in Bermuda in April?" the old lady says.

The young man laughs nastily, a sort of bark. "I've never been to Bermuda," he says, looking into his coffee.

The young woman says, "It's always nice in Bermuda, in April." She is talking to the young man. "Susan goes every April; she says it's the loveliest time." And then, fatally, she includes the old lady. "Are you going there in April?"

The old lady beams, the young man frowns, the young woman pays no attention. Everywhere in Brighams there is the sound of barriers crashing. Crazy or not, here I come.

"Yes," the old lady says.

So, they're in for it.

5

. . .

Comments so far

1. Who in hell are these "young people" and why should we care?

2. Why all this fuss about getting the old lady and the young people into conversation? Why not do it in the first line: "The young couple had planned a private little lunch at Brighams when suddenly an old lady leaned over and said . . ."

3. Bermuda? This old lady? Well then, how are you going to work in the young man's suicide, the young woman's plunging that knife into his skinny hairy chest?

Responses

1. They are Jean and John. Or Helen and Richard. Or (give them a nationality, a race) Maureen and Adrian. Yes, call them Maureen and Adrian. Adrian could be anything

and the name will go with his pretensions. (He has pretensions? Well, he has them now. Is that why his wife, this Maureen, wants to plunge the knife into his chest? For pretensions, and for other things. Is he totally unsympathetic? No, of course not. So, are you abandoning the story of the old lady after all, and concentrating on Maureen and Adrian? Hmmmm.)

2. Yes, too much fuss about getting the old lady to talk to them. Correct that. Open with the last paragraph of section #1: "Ask for some more," the old lady says across the booth divider, etc. etc. Cut whatever can be cut. Cut to the bone.

3. Bermuda is the problem. So is suicide and/or murder. (Could she, the old lady, have committed murder? Is this Poe? Is this a story? In a story, *anything* can be brought together with suicide and/or murder.)

6

. . .

"Yes," the old lady says. "April fourteenth. For nine days. And I'll be glad to get the hell out of all this snow. Have you ever seen anything like this snow? And of course they don't clean it off the streets. You don't get any public services these days. I worked in public-school education all my life and I've never seen the public services so bad as they are today. I've got a friend, Judge Baker, over in city hall, and he says the same thing. In my place, where I live, the super doesn't give a good goddamn. The snow is never shoveled off the walks; I could break a leg just trying to get out for my meals, but do you think he cares? And upstairs they're young people who don't come home till late and then they put on their stereo and play football. I tell you, it's awful. The super, he lives in the basement, you know, the cellar, and he doesn't hear the noise. I'm getting out.

I've got to get out. But I'm in luck because my friend, Judge Baker, fixed it for me to get into the Melrose Senior Housing. So that's that. I've told you all my troubles. You'll think I'm a crazy old lady who just goes on raving. Are you from here? The both of you?"

Adrian smiles.

Maureen says, "I'm from here, my husband isn't."

"Oh, is that so? You look Irish; I noticed that before I spoke to you. I could see in the mirror. Are you?"

"Uh-huh."

"From Ireland?"

"No. I was born here. My mother was from Ireland."

"Well, you could be too, you've got that face, you know. And you," she says to Adrian, "you don't look Irish."

"I'm not," he says.

"You look Jewish."

There is the suggestion of a pause here. (Make it menacing?)

"I am Jewish."

"Well, that's all right too."

Adrian laughs. Maureen shakes her head. "Why do you do that?" she says. It is one of the things she hates about him; he suspects prejudice everywhere; he's out to crush it even where it doesn't exist. To the old lady, Maureen says, "He's not Jewish, he's just pulling your leg."

"Well, he could be," she says. "He looks Jewish."

This makes Adrian laugh. He is in rather a good humor now. She is only a harmless old bore, she's feisty. She's not going to go gentle into any good night. And she swears well too. Not off-putting as it should be in an old lady.

"It's your beard," she says. "You look like one of the people in that painting, *The Last Supper.*"

"Judas?" Adrian says.

Everybody laughs. They have all settled in now for a chat. They're feeling comfortable, except for Maureen, who is studying the old lady in the mirror.

"You said you were going to Bermuda," Adrian says.

"You bet," she says. "I might even look around for a boyfriend."

"A boyfriend?" Maureen decides to throw in her lot with them.

"Sure. Why not? I'm not dead yet. Right? I don't want a lot of romance, you know, not going to bed and all, but I'd like some company, somebody to take a walk with, you know. Just have a good time."

"Well, good for you," Maureen says.

Adrian laughs.

"Now, you'd make a nice couple. Are you two married?"

"Yes."

"Yes, but . . ." (*Problem:* should he say, "Yes, but we're planning on getting a divorce"?)

"I didn't think you were married. He's laughing too much. When they're married a long time, they don't laugh like that."

Maureen and Adrian look at each other significantly.

"I've been married. He's dead now, God rest his soul. We were night and day. Complete opposites. I always loved to travel and to go to parties and have lots of people around. But not him. The one thing he liked to do, just about the only thing was to go up to Nova Scotia—that's where he was from, he was a Canuck—to go up there and sit on a rock by the water and smell the breeze. I mean, he didn't even look at the view, not that there was much to look at, but he'd just smell the air. He'd close his eyes. Other men would fish, but not him. He'd just sit there. What a man."

(Problem: where to interrupt this? Where to insert what is going on with Maureen and Adrian? But the old lady has the floor and will not relinquish it.)

"Well, he's been dead seven years now and . . ."

(She will have to be interrupted anyhow. Because too many things are going on at once. One old lady, who does not matter anyway, cannot be allowed with her silly pointless chatter to keep the reader in the dark about the suicide that is being planned, the murder that is being performed. No, the old lady must be interrupted, if not silenced. Who is she to stop the churning mills of the gods? Or even the mills of two young people, aged forty-two?

1. To Maureen it is now clear that the old lady:

    a. detested her husband,

    b. had good reasons for it,

    c. and probably killed him. She could have pushed him off that rock in Nova Scotia where he sat with his eyes closed smelling the breeze. She could have lifted another rock, a heavy one, and brought it hard down on his skull, arranging the body afterward to make it look as if he fell. No, those things never work; some smart detective, some Columbo or other, stumbles on to evidence and then she's done for. How did she kill him? Did she plunge the knife? Poison him? Or did she just wear him down, find fault, persecute him, as Adrian does to her, until he went off to his rock in Nova Scotia and died of his own accord, because death was easier than putting up with living? There is no question the old lady did it, but how?

2. To Adrian it is now clear that the old lady:

    a. detested her husband,

    b. had good reasons for it,

    c. and drove him to suicide. He was quiet, a solitary man, lost in a marriage with this itchy neurotic woman who wanted to travel and go to parties and have people about all the time. Poor bastard, he did the last thing he could to get away from her, the only thing, he put a knife to his heart and had done with it.)

Adrian and Maureen are listening to the old lady with more attention than she deserves.

"He's been dead seven years now and I've been living the way I've always wanted to. We scrimped and scraped all our lives, but now I travel and I see people and I enjoy myself. I'm living just the way I did before I was married, when I had my first love affair."

(The old lady says "love affair" in a way that leaves no doubt it was a sexual love affair. No sitting on the front-porch glider and singing songs for her. Not on your life. She says "love affair" and that's what she means: sweating on the rumpled sheets, the sounds and smells of two bodies eager to draw that special satisfaction from the other, a little blood, a little excrement, exhaustion. All these things are implicit in the way she says "when I had my first love affair.")

So.

7
. . .

In a story the narrator would have to cut out a lot of the extraneous stuff and include a lot of information we need. For instance, what's the story behind this Maureen and this Adrian? How did they get that way? Or are we supposed to believe that any married couple, aged forty-two, might go to lunch on Saturday and, in the middle of a casual conversation, plan a suicide and murder? People aren't like that. And if these people *are*, then we should be told why. We don't even know what Adrian does for a living. (Make him an engineer, self-employed. No, an architect. That's better, because he works every day with instruments surgically honed to a bright hard point. At any moment in his work he could lift his compass to his head, as if to scratch behind his ear, and insert it deftly into the ear, push a little, and zing, he is dead.) Nor do we know why he is unhappy. (Make him impotent. No, that's hackneyed. Make him obsessed with sex. No, that's silly; this is the 1980s. But his problem must be something connected with sex, because this is the 1980s. Make him frigid. Yes, *him.*) A desperate, groping man who can feel nothing except intellectually. Yes, and that is why he is an architect: he gets pleasure from form and line and mass that he can control, that he can cause to be erected. He has the ability to make blocks of living space that are completely the products of his mind. This alone makes life possible for him. Without these vicarious erections, he would die, he would commit suicide. For him to be in bed with Maureen is a horror, a denial of self, for he is left naked, with nothing except his flesh. And that is why, against his better intentions, he flays away at her at the times it will hurt most. At dinner parties, for instance, when they have guests. Yes, do you see how it is coming out? Do you see what can happen now, what must happen? They will have the party tonight. The guests will arrive, eight of them, and they will have a drink or two and then a superb dinner, because Maureen is a superb cook. She has the art of taking anything, any old piece of meat, and saucing it up in a way that makes it delicious, a feast to look at and a feast to devour. And then after dinner and after the wine, they will have brandy, and he will start on her: "Is there no coffee, dear light of my life? She is a lamp unto my feet, but she bears no coffee, alas." And the guests will laugh, or try to, and she will retreat, furious, to the kitchen to put the damned coffee on. She can't make coffee. She never has been able to. But it is not the coffee he wants; it is her capitulation. He wants her angry and hurt. (Or does he? Perhaps there is other motivation? Perhaps his inability to go on listening to himself? But why turn on her?) She is out making coffee and he is alone with his eight guests, seeking whom he may devour. He will start his isolating and crushing routine now. He will take some random remark made by a guest, by a woman even, and he will hold it up to the light, turning it back and forth slowly so that it appears in all its absurdity. He will be amusing, and the guests will laugh because after all they are guests, and then he will turn nasty, but only a little. As his nastiness sets in and his guests begin to show their displeasure, their resentment even, he will expand the circle of his malice to include whoever is foolish enough to say anything. And then he will pout or rage, whichever seems more appropriate to the moment, and in the end of course he will take it all out on her. But wait. But wait. We are already into the beginning of the final quarrel where he will commit suicide or where she will be driven finally to kill him, and we still don't know about Maureen. What does she do? Where is she from? There is no time to tell because the old lady will wait no longer. In a story she could be made to wait, at least until we can understand why Maureen, an Irish girl of some patience and sensibility, would even think of killing her husband, this tedious Adrian, but the old lady is determined to go on about her love affair.

8
. . .

"I'm living just the way I did before I was married, when I had my first love affair."

Maureen and Adrian exchange a quick glance that

the old lady catches. Adrian is about to say something, but he is interrupted by Maureen's silence; she is making a show of saying nothing. So he says nothing. Finally the silence has gone on too long.

"Oh?" he says, but the old lady has narrowed her eyes and is looking at him as if he might indeed be Judas.

"Yes," she says, and for the first time since they've begun talking she takes a sip of her coffee. If they want to hear about her love affair, they'll have to ask for it.

9
. . .

Problems

1. We still don't know about Maureen. She seems colorless, spineless even. How did she get to be forty-two? Adrian at least is a mean son of a bitch, but Maureen? She would never have married, not from the evidence here anyhow.

2. The old lady has potential, but that's all. Maybe—I don't know—maybe she *should* be crazy. At least then she'd have some style.

3. Bermuda still. Don't you ever listen? My God!

Responses

1. There's nothing to be said about Maureen. It's a fact that in some stories, the reader has to be satisfied that a character is the way he/she is. Period. (You could make Maureen a spinster type, a lonely young woman who taught school for several years on Nantucket Island; an isolated existence. She walked the rocky coast early each morning before school and then again after school, even in winter when it got dark early and a false step could have meant her life. She watched the lobstermen bring in their

catch and she watched the little fishing boats dock. And she watched as the fishermen gutted the bass and bluefish and bonito. She watched the small thick knife sink deep into the guts of the fish and then slide easily, perfectly, down to the tail. The blood was neat and thick. It smelled good. It is good for us to be here, Lord, she said, because she recited the Psalms on her morning walks. We have sat by the rivers of Babylon and we have wept because we have failed to think of Thee.) But you see, this is out of control, this is the beginning of an enormously long accounting for Maureen and it doesn't fit into a story, it bulges out, it wants to assume a life of its own. And how did she get from Nantucket Island to this unnamed Boston suburb where she is married to Adrian, an architect, who along with her is waiting for the old lady to continue her story? There is no time to say. (But what if she taught school on this island only to get away from a hideous home situation, in which her five brothers had fled to their own hideous nests and left her to cope with a mother dying of cancer and a father who drank himself into a coma each night? What if, before the escape to Nantucket, she had found salvation in a psychiatrist who told her to get away, that her own life mattered, that she must flee to save it? And so she did. She left her home in Chicago, her father's florist shop, her mother's stinking bedroom, and despite the terrible burden of guilt, she got clear of it all and came to Nantucket Island. But at what cost to herself! Imagine her guilt. Imagine her anger.) But I agree, there is no time for all this and the best solution is simply to expect the reader to get along with the data he's given. She is Adrian's wife, a nice enough woman and a good cook too, and she'll fit into this as best she can. A foil to Adrian perhaps. A foil to the old lady. True, in a story she'd be made to play a part.

2. The old lady. Well, I simply disagree. Crazy ladies

may be stylish but they are not really interesting, and you have to take this one as she is, talkative and not very charming. Anyway, toward the end she'll drop out from her own inertia.

3. Yes, Bermuda, as before, does seem to be a problem. But wait. Just wait.

10
. . .

The silence has gone on altogether too long for the old lady. The two young people have attacked their sandwiches with a certain deliberate air and she herself has finished her coffee. Unless she says something pretty quick, this whole conversation could be over.

"So what are the Bermudans like, do you think?" she says.

"The men, you mean?"

"Sure, the men. Do you think I'll find a boyfriend down there?"

"I think *you* could find a boyfriend anywhere," Maureen says.

"They're all black," Adrian says, smiling. (Or should he smirk? In any case, it cannot be a pleasant remark.)

"Black. That's what I was afraid. I didn't know if they *all* were black. Mrs. Olivier, a French lady, a friend of mine, is going too and she warned me about the black ones. She says there was this black fellow a couple of years ago who lured young girls, white girls, visitors you know, and then he killed them. Stabbed them, he did, with this long knife they have for cutting sugarcane or something. Well, I'll keep clear of that kind."

(Scene for the old lady in Bermuda: she buys a hat with a large brim and little seashell decorations. She buys several ashtrays for her friends; they are really seashells with a decal that says "Bermuda" in red, white, and blue. She is carrying a straw purse with seashells on it in the form of flowers. She is the American lady, old and ripe, looking for trouble in Bermuda. She walks along the beach and thinks of adventure. She takes off her sandals to feel the gritty sand and the cold water. And then, suddenly, before her is a thatched hut that contains a bar and a crude wooden dance floor. She sits on a stool alone and, in the mirror over the bar, watches the tall stringy black men dance. She says to the bartender, "A mai-tai, please; light on the coconut." A black man approaches and stands directly behind her, his legs spread and his hands on his hips. He is staring at her in the mirror and she is staring back at him. He blocks out her view of the dancers. She can see only him, his broad shoulders with that white cloth sticking to them, his black chest exposed by the deep neck of his shirt. He is ageless, he is smiling. At his waist he wears a crimson sash and tucked into it is a long broad knife, the kind that is used for cutting sugarcane. He smiles and smiles and his white teeth catch the light from the dim lamps, for it is night now, and she gets off the stool and follows him alone along the dark beach.)

Problem: whose scene for the old lady *is* this? The old lady's? Adrian's? Maureen's?

"Anyway," the old lady says, "I'm working on a boyfriend right here. George Murphy? Do you know him?"

They only look at her.

"He's a selectman. Or he was. He's in his seventies now. He goes by here every day and looks in. He hates women. He hates me, even though he's never met me. I said to my friend, the Judge, I said, 'Look, tell him to come in and sit down, I'm not going to eat him, and I'll buy him

a nice lunch. Soup and a sandwich. And I'll pay for it.'
That's all right these days, you know, with Women's Lib.
But he won't come in. He's afraid of women. He was mar-
ried once though. Maybe that's why."

They are abstracted, more than half gone from her.
The old lady goes on about George Murphy. He is fine-
looking even though he's lost his hair. He's a nice dresser;
she likes a nice dresser; it's important when a man gets old
to keep himself up. She goes on and on until, to them, she
is only a voice, disembodied.

Maureen is no longer with her. And Adrian is no
longer with her. They are deep in their argument after
their party tonight. The guests have gone home at last; it
seemed they would never leave.

Problem: we still don't know why Maureen married him,
how she ever could have married him.
Response: there is no time. There is no time.

Maureen has washed the makeup from her face and
has put on her nightgown. She is sitting at the long vanity
table creaming her face. In the mirror, she sees Adrian
standing behind her at the door, hands on hips, staring not
at her but at her image in the mirror. She sees his broad
shoulders with that white cloth sticking to them, his chest
with its black hair exposed by the deep neck of his pajamas. His hands are on his hips; he is smiling, smirking;
he seems ageless and evil. She looks to his waist for the
crimson sash she knows will be there and, tucked into it,
the long broad knife. Is it there? Her head reels and she
cannot see. Does he have a knife?

Problem: we must know why Maureen married him. This is
an absolutely essential piece of information.
Response: because his needs were more pitiful than her own.

Because he was more frigid than she. Because the coldness of her flesh could somehow warm the coldness of his. *Problem:* does he hate the body that much? Does she? *Response:* he does not know the body. She does not know the body. They are mere innocents, and therefore dangerous.

In the mirror she watches him and he watches her image as she reaches into the top drawer of the vanity table where, for how many years now, she has concealed a thin white knife.

She continues looking into the mirror and this is what she sees. She sees Maureen clutch the knife too low on the handle. The blade cuts deep into her palm but she does not mind, because it is doing its work as she rises and spins and in one frightful downward motion plunges the knife into his right side, between the third and fourth ribs. The knife knocks hard against bone and then slips sideways and in. It is home.

But something is wrong with time and so Adrian—with no knife in him at all, yet—is still standing at the door, waiting. In the mirror he watches Maureen's image reaching into the top drawer of the vanity table where, as he has known for many years now, she conceals a thin white knife, and this is what he sees. He sees Adrian draw the long knife from his crimson sash and hold it out, he sees her hands fly to her mouth, he sees her eyes widen in disbelief. He know that, yes, it must happen. Slowly, carefully, he inserts the knife into his right side, between the third and fourth ribs.

But now, suddenly, time resumes its ordinary way, where things happen in sequence and every action has its consequence. And so Maureen gasps as the knife strikes home. Adrian cries out once at the pain and once more at the sight of his blood. There is no question that the knife is entering his body, has entered it, but in whose hands is that knife? Who drives that blade so deep?

They know only that it is happening, now, at last.

Disembodied, somewhere, a voice is talking about a boyfriend and George Murphy and Bermuda.

Adrian's dead body slumps to the floor and Maureen stands above it, her hands over her mouth, waiting for whatever it is that she will feel, waiting for those death screams that go on and on and on.

11

. . .

Comment: this can never be a successful story. You have a murder, or maybe it's a suicide, but no story. What is missing is the creative act.

THE PRIEST'S WIFE

Thirteen Ways of Looking

at a Blackbird

1

• • •

The priest and his wife were seen skiing together before they were married; or, rather, she was seen skiing and he was around, somewhere.

She took the lift to the slope reserved for advanced skiers. She was wearing a black parka and formfitting ski pants, also black. Her blond hair hung loose and straight.

Those who watched with binoculars from the deck of the lodge said it was an exercise in discipline. She allowed herself none of the indulgences of the advanced skiers. She plunged straight down vertical slopes, shooting off at an angle over horizontal ones, slaloming between invisible poles even when her momentum would have seemed to indicate certain disaster. She never shifted weight suddenly from one leg to the other. She never skidded, never fell. She crouched, swerved, straightened, her body always completely in control.

An exercise in grace, someone said. No one could take eyes off her and so no one was sure who said it. It may have been the priest.

Snow had begun to fall, so they all went indoors for hot buttered rum and a little fooling around by the fireplace. Every now and then somebody would look out the window and see her mounting once more that precipitous slope, and then the lightning descent, the perfect turn around the invisible poles.

Among twenty snowy mountains she was the only moving thing.

2
. . .

After he met her the priest was of three minds regarding what he ought to do. After he watched her skiing on the slopes he was of one mind. He wanted to be a poet and write perfect love songs. For God, naturally. And then eventually perhaps for publication. And finally just to create a good thing. To make something. He was of one mind about that.

With such an attitude, it was inevitable that in time he got out and left behind him the order, the priesthood, and—he sometimes thought—common sense. Burdened with an artist's drive and a priest's training, he did what anyone would do. He married her and became a teacher of high school English.

3

. . .

She had a face like a woman in a novel. Her grandfather said that to her once when she was nine or ten, and it pleased her. It gave her an existence out there, in the real world, in a book.

She was Katharine Stone, age nine or perhaps ten, and she was called Kate. Her father was a psychiatrist and her mother was a psychiatric nurse; they employed a cleaning woman, a part-time gardener, and a part-time cook. These people, and her German shepherd, Heidi, were her serious world. Her play world was at school where nothing was serious, really, not for a girl who had a face like a woman in a novel.

When Kate grew up she scrutinized novels, old ones particularly, in an effort to discover what her grandfather had meant. When she grew up some more, she turned to psychology in an effort to discover which woman in which novel she might be. In time she came to know certain women well, in and out of novels.

Even though she knew she was not beautiful, she worried that she might be Anna Karenina, a woman she knew by instinct, a woman she feared. Anna, with her red leather bag, getting on the train at the beginning; Anna, with that same red leather bag, plunging beneath the train's wheels at the end. Why the red leather bag? Why the train? Surely Anna's fate was in some way connected to the fact of her face. Surely one day she would unravel what that mysterious connection might be.

Perhaps she should write a novel of her own, as Cora had told her to. Perhaps she would someday. In the meanwhile she entered the convent. It was autumn, and as the sisters walked in twos from chapel to school, the wind caught their veils and whirled them about so that they flapped like the wings of blackbirds.

4

•   •   •

Cora Kelleher had been the cleaning lady for the Stones ever since Kate's birth. She had seen Kate Stone grow up plain and skinny, she had seen her enter the convent, and she had seen her come out ten years later, blond and beautiful. In jig time Kate had gotten herself a husband, a job with IBM, and had taken up skiing, would you believe. There was no sign Kate was pregnant or about to be. Cora herself had had seven.

"I don't see she's pregnant," Cora said to Eunice, the part-time cook.

"Who would that be, now?" Eunice said, moony as ever.

"Kate Stone that was." She snorted. "The priest's wife."

"A lot of them today use the pill."

"A lot of them today use a lot of things."

"She's a beautiful girl, though." Eunice stopped peeling potatoes and gazed out the window dreamily. "And her a nun once."

"Her a nun and now that marriage. There's no luck on that marriage, let me tell you that."

"He teaches school," Eunice said, peeling again.

"Only high school. For all his priest education, he only teaches high school."

"She's a beautiful girl, though."

"Well, she was a plain stick of a thing when she was little. I remember once when she was no bigger than this, she says to me, giving herself airs, she says, 'Grandpa said I have the face of a woman in a novel.' 'And why is he telling you grand things like that?' I says. 'Because I asked him if he thought I was pretty,' she says. So I told her, I says to her, 'Well then, you'll have to write it yourself. There are no novels about skinny little things like yourself,' I says."

"Beautiful hair she has," Eunice said, peeling.

"She was always uppity. Another time, after her grandpa died it was, she said to me, all serious and with her eyes big, she says, 'I'm going to practice dying. Like Grandpa. I'm going to spend my whole life getting ready.' 'Are you, now!' I says to her. I says, 'Well, you're going to die anyway, ready or not, once it's your time.' Uppity she was and uppity she is."

"And her a nun once," Eunice said. "I could have been a nun once. Of course it's too late now." And she ran the water loudly, so Cora Kelleher had to shout.

"There'll be no luck to that marriage, you mark my words! A man and a woman are one thing. But a priest and a woman? It's like having a buzzard sitting right square on your tombstone."

5

. . .

It had been one hell of a day for him at school. The kids had been maliciously thickheaded and they had talked all through his exposition of Yeats's "Second Coming." So what was the use? And in the two hours before Kate got home from her office, he had accomplished absolutely nothing. The poem simply wouldn't come right, he just didn't have it, he wasn't a poet.

"You are a poet," she said, "you're a wonderful poet. Why don't you let me take a poet to dinner? Anywhere you want. Or you take me. Either way I get to dine with a poet. Bewitching."

So they went out to dinner and afterward to a movie and by then he'd cheered up and they made love. Kate had office work to do but she kept quiet about it and, for his sake, pinched and poked him until he felt like doing it again. After the second time they lay, exhausted, staring at the ceiling.

"I'm going to take one more try at that poem," he said.

"Good for you," she said. "And I'm going to take a shower and fix you a nice drink—I won't disturb you—and then I'll go do a little work too."

He heard the water come on and the glass doors slide closed. She was being awfully good; she always was. And he knew what a bore he must be, what a pain in the ass about being a failed poet. And God knows, he didn't mean to rage; he just couldn't help it. He'd make it up to her and surprise her in the shower.

He opened the bathroom door softly, though there was no need for stealth since the water was running wildly. He was about to slide open the glass doors to the shower when he saw—as if in a film—the long line of her body, complete, perfect. She had her head back so that the water struck her full in the face. He traced the long neck to where it disappeared in the rise of her small breasts. And then the rib cage and her little belly and the long severe thighs. Perfection.

He sat down on the toilet seat, his head in his hands.

"Will I ever know her?" he whispered, and then again, "Will I ever know her?" He had folded that body so completely into his own so many times now during these past three years, and still he had never seen her . . . he could not find the words . . . her naked face. "I will never know her," he whispered, but already he was thinking something else. He was thinking, I will never be a poet. Never.

He left the bathroom, angry, and went to his little study off the kitchen. Kate had shopped everywhere to get him just the right desk and she had decorated the study according to his instructions, but still he never used it. His desk was heaped with books and papers, so there was no room to write. He wrote either at the dining table, which he also kept heaped with books, or sitting in his easy chair. "You don't need a study if you can't write anyhow," he had told her, though it was he who had insisted on the study in the first place.

He could hear her tiptoeing around the kitchen as she got his drink ready. How could he concentrate knowing she might interrupt him at any second? "I don't want to bother you but . . ." He sat there, daring her. She glided into the room on her soft slippers and placed the drink on a coaster near him, patting him twice on the shoulder.

"God dammit," he shouted, "I'm trying to write. Is there no place in this goddamned apartment I can work in peace?"

"I didn't say anything," she said, defensive, used by now to these outbursts. "I just gave you your drink."

"You bumped me on the shoulder. You poked me twice. I was just getting it right and you interrupted and now it's gone." He looked at her with hatred and then took a good slug of his drink. "I'm sorry. I hate to sound like a bastard, but Jesus Christ!" He had been penitent for a second and now he was furious all over again. He slammed down the glass and the liquor sloshed onto his papers. "You always do this! You always ruin it! You always . . ." But she had gone. He followed her into the bedroom where she had her papers spread on the bed. She bent over the papers, not looking at him.

"Don't," she said. "Not again. I can't take it."

"Sometimes I detest you," he said. "Sometimes I curse the day I ever laid eyes on you."

She stared back at him in silence. And then she said, "Someday you'll say one thing too many. I give you warning. Now."

He backed out of the room. Several drinks later he woke her up. "Forgive me, sweet. Katie, forgive me, please," he said, and buried his head in her breasts.

"I know," she said. "It's all right. I love you."

"Friends?" he said.

"Friends," she said.

And so it was over, this time.

6

. . .

They had been married five years now, and it was winter. Icicles filled the long window that looked out over the ruined garden. It was evening and shadows in the garden and shadows in the living room flickered as Kate moved back and forth in front of the light, watering the indoor plants. She wore a red gown, knotted at the neck and waist, and it created for her a mood in which she could feel withdrawn but not unpleasant. Her husband sat with his chin in his hands, watching her, watching the shadows she cast. He had just despaired, yet again, of ever being a poet. And besides, he had a terrible sore throat. And so they had their last fight.

It was about her habit of visiting her widower father, that bastard, every Saturday, and about her job at IBM. And it was about her way of being vague with him, as if what he said required only half her attention, as if he didn't really matter. And it was about his failure as a writer.

Five years of this and now, at last, she had had enough.

"I can't live your life for you," she said. "There are some things you've got to do for yourself. You've got to breathe, you've got to eat, you've got to crap, and god dammit, you've got to live. And if you hate your job, then do something about it. And if you resent mine, which you do, then why don't you . . ."

"Go ahead, say it! Say it! You've been wanting to."

But she didn't say it. She went to bed and he went to the kitchen for a drink. He had a second and a third and then he went in to wake her but she wasn't asleep yet anyhow. He apologized and she apologized and it was almost over.

Deliberately he looked at her hand. He had had a sort of vision once of who she was and how she loved him and it had split him down the middle. He had thought at the time that he had become two people, both of them crazy. And all because of her hand. She had placed it on his knee during a quarrel—afterward he could not remember what the quarrel was about—and he had watched it crumple and break like an autumn leaf, while his words continued angry and smooth and satisfying. In those days he had had all the words. And then, as the hand fell from his knee, he stopped and said to her, "I'm not a good person. I'm not like you." He cried then, and he had not cried in fifteen years. That was during the first week of their marriage.

Now, five years later, he sat on the edge of the bed looking at her hand, white and small with long tapered fingers, trying to make it happen again, that vision.

But nothing happened.

"Friends?" he said.

"Friends," she said.

In bed, they both pretended to sleep. After a long while she got up and poured herself a drink and sat in the dark living room. She finished it and poured herself another. Then, not really knowing what she was going to do, she put on the light and got out a pencil and a legal pad and wrote, "I want out. I want a divorce." She stared at the words for a long time, and then she wrote them again.

And then again. She found a peculiar satisfaction in form-
ing the letters, in putting down on paper those words that
finally said the unsayable. "I hate him. I hate what he
turns me into. I hate the way he hates himself." She made
a list of the things she could not say, and she said them.
She wrote out their most violent quarrels, including in pa-
rentheses the words she had not said because they might
kill him. ("You'll never be a poet." "You have a gift for
words but no gift for poetry." "You're wrecking your life
and you're trying to wreck mine, but I'm not going to let
you." "Why didn't you stay in the priesthood and just
drink yourself to death?") And it was astonishing. Words
did not kill, at least not on paper. Rather, they gave her a
wonderful feeling of release, of freedom. She got herself
another drink and went on writing until, hours later, she
had run out of things she was angry at. Without a pause
she moved into a description of how she had first met him,
her husband now, in the train station. The strap had broken on her red leather tote bag and he had offered to help
her with it. But the bag was square, and with his hands
occupied with skis and his own suitcase, he hadn't been
able to get a good grip on it; he dropped it and it opened
and spilled out keys and makeup and God knows what else.
She had laughed at him then and he had laughed too.

She stopped writing—these notes, in time, would find
their way into her first novel—and looked out at the garden
where the sun was just touching the silver branches of the
trees. A single blackbird lit on the end of a branch, making
it bend, sending down a thin sifting of snow. Smiling to
herself, she recited the Magnificat, as she had done every
morning for the past twenty years.

And so the divorce was put off for eleven months.

7

. . .

During those eleven months they often walked by the river together. And they often dined out. He appeared to be the more talkative but in public she did most of the talking. If the marriage was not a happy one, they at least put a good face on it, and five years is a long time to put a good face on anything.

Acquaintances who had known them off and on for years said that marriage made them both merely conventional. His wild imagination and flights of whimsy disappeared altogether, replaced by a kind of watchfulness and a mildly sardonic humor. She talked politics a lot and, when the conversation turned to religion, she avoided discussion of how much she still believed, dismissing the topic with a remark about how bored she was with Sunday sermons.

Friends of hers who visited from the convent said the couple was supremely happy. She had taken to wearing high-fashion clothes, finding it necessary to be more feminine now that she had so many males directly responsible to her. She had a big job with big obligations. Friends of his who visited from the monastery said she had done wonders for him. He had put on weight and he was no longer so volatile. He had settled down to being a high school teacher; her big job with IBM obviously posed no ego problems for him.

They had private jokes and sometimes on the street they were caught laughing immoderately. They held hands at these times. They also held hands in restaurants, though not so frequently as on their walks. This was not natural in people married so long; it was probably a cover-up for something.

After eleven endless months they separated.

8

• • •

In the two years of their separation he had seven job promotions with his ad agency and she wrote two novels, both of them flops.

He had moved to New York, and by some fluke, or by talent, managed to put together a trendy portfolio. In no time he was making as much money as Kate, and by the end of the two years he was making a great deal more. He was happy and fulfilled, except of course that he missed her. He was a different man now. It was the writing that had made him so miserable. She'd see. Would she take him back? Would she agree to drop the divorce business and give the marriage another try? And, ahem, would IBM be willing to transfer her from her new job in Gaithersburg to a newer one in New York?

She smiled. She would think about it. But he'd better be clear on one thing: she was fiddling around with a novel and she didn't intend to give it up for anybody. Got that?

The first two novels were mistakes, no doubt about it. She had begun with a description of their meeting in the train station, a nice, tightly written scene, but when read aloud it sounded so like a murder mystery that she decided to turn it into one. She killed herself off in the first chapter and then . . . well, it didn't work out. Her murders were clumsy and her murderers uninteresting; she was more preoccupied with psychoanalyzing the bereaved than with moving the damned plot along. Five publishers turned it down before she realized that it was a mistake, that she just didn't know anything about murders and she didn't care much either.

With the second novel she decided to stick to what she knew: life in a convent. She put in the mistress of novices and her more colorful teachers and her eager and ambitious nun friends, all of them meticulously drawn. She had gotten down every revealing gesture, every idiosyncrasy of speech and behavior, and yet somehow nobody came alive. The book was a jumble of real people rather than fictional characters, and it was rejected everywhere.

Her next novel, the one she wouldn't give up for anybody, would be different. She would write about what she knew as if she didn't really know it. And she would put herself in it. One thing was certain: whatever it was that she knew and was able to get down on paper, she herself was involved in it.

Meanwhile she would think about dropping the divorce suit. She might even think about requesting a transfer.

9

. . .

In Utica, New York, the priest's mother heard the following established facts at the Ladies' Guild:

1. Katharine Stone had grown up in Utica and moved to Boston when she was five. She was an airline stewardess for seven years and often flew back and forth between Boston and upper New York State. Now that she was separated she had gone back to United. She had been seen in her uniform only last week. In Utica. Many people in Utica knew her well.

2. Kate Stone was a staff editor of *Ms.* magazine and had formerly been a fashion model. She was six feet tall and beautiful. She dated married men.

3. Katharine Stone was a former nun who grew up in D.C. but who lived, at the time of her marriage, in Baltimore. She was from a distinguished family of doctors in which all the men went to Harvard and all the women to

Radcliffe. She was, despite this, not the least bit snobbish and was quite content teaching high school English. Her family would never permit a divorce.

4. A friend of the guild's president's daughter had gone to Noroton with Kate Stone and there they had both known the Ford girls, Anne and Charlotte. They, the four, had not been close since she entered the convent. Kate Stone, of course. Anne Ford had not entered the convent and neither had Charlotte.

5. Kate Stone had been a dancer until she broke her foot. Since then she had worked for IBM and spent all her free time skiing. She was going to get a divorce and then marry her ski instructor.

The priest's mother went home and cried until ten, when "Kojak" came on.

10

. . .

In the spring of that year they both got transfers to Boston, where they bought a house and took up where they left off, only a lot better. Kate was involved in writing her novel and her husband was all worked up over a new ad campaign, and so they were happy. They even put in their names to adopt a child.

That summer they drove to Baltimore to visit Kate's friends in the convent. Kate was all in white and very tanned though it was still only the end of June. He was wearing his white suit and his white shoes, too summery perhaps, just this side of affectation. They knew they looked good.

Kate's friends came to the visiting parlor in twos and threes. Visits were not so exciting as they had been years ago, before the cloister had moved into the world. These days a visit from outside meant little. Still, everybody was curious to see the couple now that they were reconciled. How long would it last? Kate looked wonderful, but he was putting on weight. He was polite, said very little. Whenever they asked about him, he answered briefly and directed the conversation back to Kate and her friends. There was no telling from the way he acted whether or not he'd take off again for New York. Poor Kate.

At noon some of the sisters went to chapel for midday meditation. Kate and her husband went for a walk around the grounds. Hand in hand they walked down the long slope of grass to the lake. A small dirt path ran around the lake and they followed it for a while, disappearing among the overhanging willows and high swamp grass. There were pine needles everywhere. He wanted to lie down on them but she said no, it was time to turn back. They lay down for a little while anyway.

As they came out from under the trees, they paused and looked across the lake. The sun turned the water green and cast a green reflection on their faces and clothes.

The sisters, coming out of chapel, paused on the cloister walk to gaze out over the lake. The sisters saw the man and woman, their hands joined together, their clothes of dazzling white drenched green in the reflection from the lake. Just those two white figures, joined, against the world of green.

Someone cried out in disbelief.

11
. . .

And so she finished the damned book, as she said, and got a publisher, and sold 1,600 copies of it. *The New York Times* said it was a promising start and *The New Republic* said it was witty and disturbing. Nobody else said anything about it.

What she wrote was, in actuality, a pack of lies about her friends at IBM and about her husband and—in a peculiar way—about herself. The characters numbered thirteen and they were as diverse in their morals and desires and preoccupations as even God or nature would have made them. There was a man who was so insecure he dared to communicate with his employees only when he had worked himself into a rage. There was a man whose sole love was for machines and who had cut himself off from human intercourse completely. There was a housewife whose loneliness and vulnerability drove her into affairs with any man who presented himself. And another who wanted to write poetry and instead was drinking herself to death. And a woman executive who made passionate love to her husband each night, moaning and tearing at his flesh, and then went to the bathroom where she calmly and coldly masturbated before the full-length mirror. They were unscrupulous people and hateful people and pitiful people. And all of them, so her husband recognized, understanding at last, were Kate Stone. In some way, at some moment in the story, they all wore her face.

He was grateful for the book. She existed now, in reality, for him.

She was grateful too. The book was done, some kind of awful duty was discharged, and she felt no desire to write another. All she wanted to do now was to take up skiing once again and to conquer at last the dark fear of hers that plunging down that slope was somehow entering the valley of the shadow of death.

12

. . .

It was their anniversary and she gave him a card she had made herself. Inside it she had written, "This river that carries us with it, out of control, out of any control, at least carries us together."

He did not know what she meant, he never knew what she meant, but it no longer mattered because he had seen her naked face and loved her.

13

. . .

Time passed for them. There may have been children, a boy and a girl, adopted. There may have been a dog. There may have been . . . but the snow falls and everything recedes into uncertainty, except that we die and we do not wish to die.

"It's snowing," she said.

"And it's going to snow," he said.

The light on the snow had been pale purple all afternoon and, though it continued to snow, she insisted nonetheless on going skiing.

They were seen leaving the lodge where everyone was sitting around drinking hot buttered rum by the fireplace and they were seen again later taking the lift to the highest slope. Slowly at first, and then with lightning speed, they descended, two black figures against the white snow, darting across one another's path, plunging straight down and then veering off at an angle, dodging invisible poles. For a long while people from the lodge watched them, but then the sun dipped behind the trees. Nonetheless they went on ascending and descending that hill.

In the first dark an owl hooted and some winter bird shifted on his perch in the cedar limbs.

MYSTERIES

CONSOLATIONS OF
PHILOSOPHY

Mr. Kirko was taking his time dying in bed number seven. He just kept lying there week after week.

"Not even getting any worst. At least not to the naked eye," said his daughter Shelley. "Look, I've got obligations, the children," she said.

"Obligations we've all got," her brother Mervin said. "You've got obligations. Angel's got obligations. And my obligations you know. I'm the son. So forget your obligations sometime. It's Papa."

"It's too true. It's Papa," said Angel, who was unmarried and had nothing. "He's all I've got," Angel said.

"And *he's* dying," Shelley said.

The orderlies came hollering "Beds number seven and eight" and pulled the curtains around to make tents. Then they staggered off with Mr. Kirko and bed number eight to give them baths. These were old orderlies and their backs didn't straighten much anymore, so they just put Mr. Kirko and bed number eight in the water and let them sit there. Then these orderlies broke out the old Camels and smoked while the sick people sat in hot water till their behinds shriveled.

"This is how it is when you're one of the masses," one said.

"Rome wasn't built in a day," the other said.

Then one said a lot and the other said a lot and they checked to see if Mr. Kirko's behind was shriveled, and it was, so they got their hooks under his armpits and dragged him out of the tub. He groaned and his eyes rolled up, but at least he didn't die on them. They sat him on a three-legged stool to dry him. The stool scraped on the tile floor.

"Hear that noise?" Mr. Kirko asked.

They stopped toweling him because he never spoke and now he was speaking.

"That's the springs in my ass, breaking."

He threw up then, yellows and browns, and most of it went into his slipper.

"Goddamned pigs when they get old."

"There's no fool like an old fool."

These orderlies slammed his foot into the slipper and propped him against the wall. His face was all red from his bath and his foot was yellow and brown.

They checked to see if bed number eight's behind was shriveled, and it was, so they got their hooks into him and started to drag, but he wouldn't give. They let him have a little punch in the head to show they meant business, but it didn't do any good because he only gave a moan or two and died.

"Well, naught is certain save death and taxes."

"We'll let this sleeping dog lie."

They staggered back to bed number seven with Mr. Kirko. The son, Mervin Kirko, was pacing up and down outside the room, looking at his watch. Angel Kirko, who had nothing, was standing in the corner twisting her handkerchief. Shelley Kamm was looking through her purse and sighing a lot.

"Did we have a nice bathie-poo?" Shelley said to her father as these orderlies pulled the curtains.

"It's little enough to have," Angel said.

Inside the tent the orderlies rested for a while and then they each took an arm of Mr. Kirko and counted down. "Three, two, one, GO!" And Mr. Kirko went thundering up onto the bed, headfirst. His head went shlunk into the wall. He wailed for a minute and then tuned down to whine.

They threw back the curtains and approached the weeping women.

"It's an ill wind that blows no good," one said.

"It's too true," Angel said.

"It's a mercy some of them go when their time has come," the other said.

"I know you're doing everything you can," Shelley said.

On the way out these orderlies nodded at good old Mervin.

"You can just pace around," they said. "Up and down, back and forth, you name it."

Angel and Shelley didn't know what to do next.

"He doesn't look any worst to me," Shelley said.

"Not to the naked eye, he doesn't," Angel said.

"Oh, nurse, nurse," Shelley said, calling Nurse Jane. "He doesn't look any worst, does he?"

"Well, he's going to be," Nurse Jane said. "They don't just go in and out of here unless they're seriously, you know. What he needs is some needles and bottles, some pickies and pokies, and a tube up his nose."

Nurse Jane returned with everything she promised.

"Bed number eight," she said to Angel. "Where is he?"

"Personally, I don't know," Angel said. "I haven't the slightest."

"She hasn't the slightest," Shelley said. "She's never had anything and now she's losing her papa."

"It's a matter of professionalism," Nurse Jane said. "There are lists to be filled out, tags, markers, numbers, identity bands, indicators, thingamabobs, you have no idea. So you can't just have bed numbers disappearing. So you've got to tell me everything you can about this case. Now you, Miss Kirko, when did you last see bed number eight?"

"Well, I'll do my best," Angel said. "He was last seen by me personally when they staggered him off for his bath."

"Bath," Nurse Jane said and stalked away, kachung, kachung. "Very good," she said a few minutes later. "Very good, Miss Kirko. We found him dead in the bath and so he's accounted for." She leaned across Shelley and put her hand gently on Angel's bosom. "It's just so we know," she said tenderly. "We have to know."

"It can't be easy," Angel said.

"It's the children I worry about," Shelley said.

"When the doctor comes, you'll see," Nurse Jane said, and wheeled the empty bed out of the room.

The doctor appeared at seven o'clock on the bonker. He had a clipboard in his hand and he kept looking from it to the place where bed eight used to be.

"I see they've dispatched bed eight," he said. "You must be the Kirkos. You belong to bed seven."

"Yes, we're the Kirkos," Mervin said. "I'm the son and these are the two daughters, Angel Kirko and Shelley

Kamm. Shelley was a Kirko before she was a Kamm."

"How do you do," they all said, shaking everything.

"I'm Dr. Robbins," Dr. Robbins said.

"Dr. Robbins," they all said, grateful as anything.

Angel and Shelley took a good long look at Dr. Robbins while he took a good long look at Mr. Kirko. In each arm old Kirko had needles that ran down from bottles full of white and bottles full of yellow, and there was a tube up his nose that went somewhere and another tube that ran from his winkler into a bottle under the bed. Mr. Kirko was getting the full treatment.

"You're very young for a doctor," Shelley said, taking in the little bulge in his white pants.

"But competent," Dr. Robbins said.

"Oh, I didn't mean," Shelley said.

"We never meant," Angel said.

"Of course, of course," Dr. Robbins said, and he bit the inside of his face so they'd know.

"I'll wait outside," Mervin said.

"You can pace up and down," Dr. Robbins said. "Or back and forth. You name it."

The doctor stood for a while looking at Mr. Kirko. He plucked at his leg; it looked like turkey.

"I think that leg's going to have to come off," the doctor said.

"Oh no!" Angel said, fainting.

"Oh, God in heaven!" Shelley said.

Angel kept on fainting.

"Mervin! Mervin! We've got to make a decision. This Dr. Robbins here says the leg has got to come off. It's our duty to decide," Shelley said.

Mervin came back in from his corridor.

"These are the moments one dreads, Doctor," Mervin said.

"Oh, no!" Angel said, fainting some more.

"Before we decide," Shelley said, "I think I should have a word with the doctor in private."

"I've never had anything," Angel said as Mervin dragged her from the room.

Shelley shut the door and leaned against it, her head thrown back. Outside she could hear them pacing up and down, back and forth.

"I thought we should have a word alone," Shelley said.

"Most understandable at a time like this, Mrs. Kamm," he said, reaching for his zipper.

"Yes, it's difficult for all of us, Doctor. It's the children I worry about." She slipped off her panties and in one graceful motion scooped them up from the floor and tucked them into her purse.

They stood for a moment looking at bed number seven.

"We could put him on the floor, Doctor. He wouldn't mind."

"It's better the patient not be disturbed," he said and gave a little tweak to a tube here and a tube there.

"Oh, dear," Shelley said.

"Now if you will please step over to the door and lean your back against it, so," the doctor said. "Very good. And now we'll lift this skirt and—yes, you'll have to bend your knees as if you were sliding down the wall, that's right—and then I'll just slip this in here. Um, we need a little wiggly, then oomph, there we are."

"Yes, that does do nicely, Dr. Robbins," Shelley said.

They stood there like a Rorschach.

"Perhaps, Mrs. Kamm, you'd prefer to put your purse on the floor."

"Oh, silly of me."

"Just drop it. That's right. And then you can put your hands right here."

"Oh," she said. "Oh."

"I think you'll find, Mrs. Kamm, that once your father's leg comes off, you'll be more than pleased you agreed to it."

"Oh, I'm sure you're right, Dr. Robbins. It's just that, you know, we've known him so long, Doctor, and always with the leg."

"Yes, yes, of course. These feelings are natural. There would be something wrong if you didn't feel them."

"Oh, yes," she said.

"Could you move that knee out a little, and away?"

"Like this?"

"Fine," he said. "Well, at least we're having marvelous weather . . . for this time of year."

"Marvelous," she said. "Doctor, I want to thank you sincerely for giving us your valuable time. We truly appreciate it."

"A doctor does his best," he said. "Comfortable?"

"Mmmm, yes. Doctor, I hope you won't think me overly personal, but I couldn't help noticing when you took it out what an enormous jumjum you have."

"Oh, I don't know," he said, shrugging modestly.

"Oh, you do, you do. Truly."

He gave her a little jab to the left.

"Thuth thuth thuth," they laughed.

"You must have gone to a wonderful medical school," she said.

"Harvard," he said. "They teach you everything."

"It must be wonderful," she said.

"Philosophy," he said. " 'Every proposition is true or false.' Langer."

"That's deep," she said.

"Heidegger," he said. " 'Listen to what is not being said.' "

"That's deep too," she said.

"Bucky Fuller," he said. " 'Everything that goes up must come down.' "

"I've heard that one," she said.

"Human behavior is a language," he said.

"Yes," she said.

"If the material of thought is symbolism, then the mind must be forever furnishing symbolic versions of its experiences," he said. "Otherwise thinking could not proceed."

"Ooh," she said, moving her right hip forward and backward in a new way.

"Perhaps I'm being too technical, Mrs. Kamm?"

"Oh no, Doctor, no. Those are beautiful thoughts," she said.

"Very well," he said. "Now, Mrs. Kamm, if you would just move this foot forward and in a bit."

"Oh!"

"You see."

There was a banging outside the door, bonka bonka bonk.

"It's Angel," Shelley said.

"If you'll concentrate, please," he said.

"Oom, oom," she said, and her feet rose from the floor.

Their bodies began to shake like dust rags, and then she bit his neck, and then he punched her ribs to make her stop. Finally she shook uncontrollably and he tore at her hair.

Bonka bonka bonk at the door.

"Hungh," he said, pulling her loose and dropping her in the corner. "Hungh," he said again and stood looking down at his ruined jumjum.

Bonka bonka bonk at the door again.

"It's me," Angel's voice said. "I want to come in."

"I'm just pacing," Mervin said from down the corridor.

Shelley brushed off her dress and patted her hair into place. "It's not bad enough about Papa," she said. "They have to make a scene in the corridor."

"It's the tension," Dr. Robbins said, all zipped and polished. He opened the door. "Come in," he said. "Your sister has reached her decision."

"The leg has got to come off," Shelley said. "Dr. Robbins is right."

"What's all this?" Angel said, pointing to the chunks of Shelley's hair with blood on the ends.

"That's my hair," Shelley said. "These decisions are never easy, Angel."

"Whatever the doctor says," Mervin said.

"I'll tell Nurse Jane," Dr. Robbins said.

In a moment the two orderlies came hollering "Bed number seven" and wheeled out the last of Mr. Kirko. It was a sad noise going.

"Man proposes, God disposes," one said.

"Every cloud has a silver lining," the other said.

Angel and Shelley and Mervin stood in the empty room looking at one another.

"Once that leg is gone it will be different."

"That leg was the trouble."

"He never looked any worst. Not to the naked eye."

"He looked worst with tubes and needles."

"And the thing in his winkler."

"There's nothing left to do but pray."

"It's too true."

A storm broke outside the window. They all went and looked at it. Rain fell like swords.

"Well, at least he's not out in that storm."

"Yes, that's a mercy."

"It's the children I worry about."

BRIEF LIVES IN CALIFORNIA

Leonora started out pretty and bright.

"She could be a movie star," her mother said, "but I would never do that to my child. I would never allow a child of mine to be in the limelight. I want Leonora to be just normal."

So Leonora took ballet and tap and piano.

"Perhaps she has other gifts," the dance teacher said. "Perhaps she has a gift for music."

The piano teacher was more to the point. "She has nothing," he said. "And she's driving me crazy."

"You could be a movie star," her mother said.

•   •   •

In junior high Leonora was one of the first to grow breasts; the other girls resented her for that. But in high school her breasts made her popular with the boys, so she didn't care about the girls. She became a cheerleader and after every game she and the other cheerleaders crowded into the booths at Dante's and waited for the team to arrive. Then they all drank Cokes and ate cheeseburgers and grabbed at one another in the booths—nothing serious, just good fun— and made out on the way home.

In November of her senior year Leonora was parked in front of her house in Chuckie's car.

"Why won't you do it?" Chuckie asked. "Everybody does."

"I don't know," she said, miserable. "I want to, but I can't. I just can't."

"Nobody saves themselves for marriage anymore. Is that what you think you're doing?"

"I think I was meant for better things," she said, not really knowing what she meant. "I mean, I get straight A's and B's."

"Ah shit," Chuckie said. "Just put your hand here. Feel this."

"No, I was meant for better things."

"But you've got to start somewhere," Chuckie said. "Hell, I'm captain of the team."

But Leonora was already getting out of the car, feeling chosen, feeling—she searched for the word—exalted. Yes, that was it. She was meant for better things.

· · ·

In the admissions office at Stanford, Leonora was a floater, somebody who hadn't yet sunk to the bottom but somebody who wouldn't get picked out of the pool unless a real Stanford freshman decided to go to Yale or somewhere. That year a lot of freshmen went to Yale and so Leonora, floating almost to the end, was admitted to Stanford.

"You could be a college professor," her mother said.

"Or a famous writer. You could win the Nobel Prize, maybe."

"Dry up," Leonora said. "What do you know about it? You never even went to college."

"Oh baby," she said. "Oh sweetheart, don't be mean to your mother, Leonora. I only want what's best for you. I only want you to be happy."

"Then dry up," Leonora said.

•   •   •

The worst part about Stanford was that they made her take freshman English. She had been among the top thirty in high school and now she was back to writing compositions. At first she had just been a little nasty to the teacher in class, to let him know how she felt about being there. But after she had written the first assigned paper, she decided to go see him and demand an explanation. He gave it to her. He explained that it was a requirement of the university that every student demonstrate a basic competence in expository writing and that she had not, in the qualifying tests, demonstrated that. And then he handed her the corrected paper.

It was covered with little red marks—diction? antecedent? obscure, no no no—and there was a large black C at the bottom of the page.

"You gave me a C," Leonora said. "I've never had a C in my life."

"There's nothing wrong with a C," he said. "It's a perfectly acceptable grade. It's average, maybe even above average."

"You gave me a C," she said and, choking on her tears, ran from his office.

Her next two papers came back with C's on them also, so she knew he was out to get her. His name was Lockhardt and he had written a couple of novels and thought he was hot shit.

Leonora went to the ombudsman and complained that she was being discriminated against. She should not have to take freshman English in the first place, and in the second place Lockhardt was guilty of unprofessional conduct in browbeating her and making her feel inferior.

The ombudsman went to the chairman of the English department who called in Lockhardt and then called in Leonora and finally checked her papers himself. The next day he told Leonora that yes, she would have to take freshman English like all the others, that the grades Professor Lockhardt had given her seemed fair enough, that he was sorry Professor Lockhardt had made her feel inferior. He told Lockhardt for God's sake go easy on the girl, she's half-crazy, and whatever you do don't be alone with her in your office. He told the ombudsman that the problem had been settled to everyone's satisfaction and there was no need to take all this to the provost. So everyone was miserable and satisfied.

Leonora's final grade was a C, all because of that bastard Lockhardt.

. . .

Patty Hearst was wrestled, struggling, into the trunk of a car in Berkeley and the next day she was headlines in all the papers. Leonora narrowed her thin eyes and thought, Why couldn't they have taken me?

. . .

In her junior year she moved in with Horst Kammer. He was clearly one of the better things that she was meant for. He was very smart and spent a lot of time with the house-master, so that in Horst she had not only a roommate, she had instant acceptance as well. Horst was too intellectual to be much interested in sex, but he didn't mind occasional sex with Leonora and that was enough for her.

Horst dressed in army fatigues and spent a lot of his time protesting Stanford's investments in South Africa. Leonora protested along with him and they were arrested together during the spring sit-in at Old Union. Leonora felt proud to be involved in something historical, something that mattered. There were over a hundred students arrested and they were each fined nearly two hundred dollars. Leonora's mother sent the money, and with it a note saying, "You're like Vanessa Redgrave or Jane Fonda. You're doing your part."

"God, that woman is hopeless," Leonora said.

.   .   .

Two photographs.

One. Leonora is home from college and all the relatives have come over for dinner. Afterwards somebody snaps an Instamatic of Leonora and her mother and father, sitting on the floor in front of the Christmas tree, surrounded by gifts. The mother and father each have an arm around Leonora and they are smiling directly into the camera. Leonora is smiling too, but she is looking off to the right of the camera, as if at the very last minute she decided the picture is not what she wants; she wants something else.

"She could be a photographer's model," her mother says, examining the picture. "She could be on all the covers."

Two. Leonora has just crested the hill on Campus Drive and is about to make the long clear descent on her new ten-speed bike. She passes two professors who are taking a noon walk, looking like anybody else, just enjoying the California spring. Leonora does not notice them, does not see that one of them is Lockhardt. She sees only the long long hill before her, and she feels the warm wind blowing through her hair. She sits high on the seat, no hands, and lifts her arms straight out from the shoulders, surrendering completely to the sun and the wind and being young and pretty, with everything, every wonderful thing ahead of her.

"Look at that girl," Lockhardt says. "God, somebody should photograph that."

 .   .   .

In her senior year, her second year with Horst, Leonora was all showered and getting ready to go to a frat party when Horst said, "Come on, let's do it." He wasn't interested in doing it that often, so she said, "I'm all ready for the party, but if you're sure you want to . . ." "I want to," he said. "I'm up for it. Look." And so he chased her from the bedroom into the living room and then back into the bedroom where she collapsed on the bed, laughing and tickling him, and they made love. "Was it wonderful?" she said. "Was it better?" "You're terrific," he said, "you're great. Where the hell is my deodorant?"

At the party everybody drank a lot of beer and tequila sunrises and after a while they got to the subject of how often you ball your roommate. When Horst's turn came, he gave a long and funny speech about the primacy of the intellect and the transitory nature of sexuality. He described the postures you get into and he made them sound new and funny, and he said the real problem is that an hour later you're still hungry for more. He had everybody with him and he was feeling really good about his performance, you could tell, and then he paused and said, anticlimactically, "Let's face it folks, what we're dealing with here is just two mucous membranes rubbing together."

Everybody laughed and applauded and spilled beer.

Horst shook his head and smiled sneakily at Leonora.

But then somebody added, "They're sebaceous membranes, actually. Get your membranes straight, Horst."

Everybody laughed even louder and Leonora laughed too and Horst saw her do it.

So he was furious and, on the way home, when Leonora leaned against his side, her head on his shoulder, Horst put his hand on her breast. He felt for the nipple and when he had it firmly between his thumb and forefinger, he twisted it suddenly and violently, pressing down with his thumbnail. Leonora screamed in pain.

"You bitch," he said. "You fucking whore. Why don't you get out of my life? You're just a nothing. You're a noose around my neck."

"No," Leonora said. "No."

.   .   .

Patty Hearst was arrested in an apartment in San Francisco. Her picture appeared in all the papers, laughing like crazy, her fist clenched in the revolutionary salute. She listed her occupation as "urban guerrilla." Leonora was done with all that now that she was done with Horst. And who cared about Patty Hearst anyhow?

.   .   .

Leonora got her diploma in June, but she had to take one more course that summer before she had enough credits to officially graduate. She signed up for creative writing, taught by "staff." But staff turned out to be that bastard Lockhardt. He didn't seem to remember her, and everybody said he was a really good teacher, and she wanted to write a novel someday, so she decided to give him another chance.

Lockhardt wasn't interested in the things that interested her. She wanted to write something different, but

Lockhardt kept talking about the initiating incident and the conflict and the characters. Old stuff. She wrote a story about a shoplifter named Horst, following him from the moment he picked up a tie until the moment he got out of the store, and she wrote it completely from within his mind, what he was thinking. Lockhardt said that the reader had no way of knowing that Horst was stealing, and that she should simply say so. But she explained that she was trying to be more subtle than that. She explained that the reader was supposed to find out Horst was stealing only after the fact, after he was outside the shop, otherwise the story would be just like any other story. They argued back and forth for a long time and then Lockhardt just shrugged his shoulders and said, "Well, I guess you've accomplished what you set out to do. Congratulations." The same thing happened with her next two stories. He didn't like them, so he said the reader couldn't follow them. He couldn't seem to understand that she was trying to do something different.

And then in August she got her grade. A flat C. She went straight from the registrar's office to Lockhardt.

"I have to speak to you," she said.

"Sit down," he said. "Have a seat. But I've got to see the dean in five minutes, so if you're going to need more than that . . ."

"You gave me a C."

"Right. I hope you weren't too disappointed."

"You," she said. "You," but the words wouldn't come out.

"Well, your work was not really extraordinary. I mean, I think you'll agree that it wasn't A work."

"It was C work, I suppose. It was only average."

"There's nothing wrong with being average. Most of us are. Most of our work is average."

She stood up and walked to the door. "What do I

care," she said. "I can live with a C." And she slammed the door behind her.

She came back late the next afternoon, she was not sure why, but she knew she had to tell him something. Lockhardt was at his desk, typing, his back to the open door, and Leonora stood there in the corridor watching him. Nobody else was around. She could kill him and no one would know she had done it. If she had a knife or a gun, she could do it. That bastard.

He kept on typing and she just stood there watching him, thinking. And then suddenly he turned around and gave a little shout. "My God, you scared me half to death."

Leonora just stared at him, and he stared back, looking confused or maybe frightened. Then she turned and walked away.

She had not told him what he had done to her, but she would someday. She'd let him know. She'd let him know.

• • •

Leonora moved to San Francisco to be on her own. She got a studio apartment with a fire escape that looked down onto the roof of the Jack Tarr Hotel and she applied for jobs at Gumps and at the St. Francis—they asked her "doing what?"—and she shrugged and said to hell with them, she had a Stanford education. But her money ran out eventually and she took a job at Dalton's selling books.

Nothing interesting ever happened at Dalton's, and besides you had to press sixty buttons on the computerized register every time you rang up a sale. The worst part was that everybody kept buying a novel called *The Love Hostage,* written by that bastard Lockhardt. After the first four sales, she refused to sell any more. "I'm on my break," she'd say and make the customer go to another register.

Leonora hated her job, hated the people she worked

with, hated books. Somewhere there must be something different happening. Even Patty Hearst, who was a zilch, a nothing, even she had things happen to her. With a name like Patty.

One night when she had worked late, Leonora decided to take a walk. She would make something happen. She moped along Polk Street to Geary and then back, but nothing happened. There were a million or so faggots eyeing each other, but nobody eyed Leonora. She went up to her studio and had a beer and then came down again and set off deliberately in the direction of Golden Gate Park. She knew what she was doing. She could be raped. She could be murdered. Lockhardt used to talk all the time about Joyce Carol Oates characters, how they set up situations for themselves, getting trapped, getting murdered, having their pink and gray brains spilled out on the sidewalk. She liked Joyce Carol Oates. She got as far as the Panhandle and was about to turn around and go home when she realized somebody was following her. For a block, then for a second block. She could hear the heels go faster when she went faster, slow down when she did. Her heart began to beat very fast and she could feel the vein in her forehead pulsing. She wanted it to happen, whatever it was. She turned around suddenly, hands on hips, her head thrown back, ready. At once the man following her crossed the street and headed in the opposite direction. Leonora walked for another hour and then went home. Would nothing happen to her, ever?

The next day she quit her job at Dalton's. They were limiting her. They were worse than Stanford.

• • •

The Women's Support Group was having a terrible time with Leonora.

"You've got to open up to your feelings as a woman," they said.

"Men have done this to you. They've refused to let you get in touch with your feelings," they said.

"What is it you feel? What is it you want?" they said.

"I want," Leonora said, "I don't know, but I think I want to die."

"No, what do you really want?" they said.

· · ·

Leonora bought a gun and a copy of *The Love Hostage* on the same day. There was no connection she could see. She wanted them, that was all. It was time.

She loaded the gun with six bullets and hid it in a Kleenex box under a lot of tissues. It was for protection in this crazy city. It was a safeguard. It was just something nice to have around.

And then she sat down to read *The Love Hostage*. From the first page she was fascinated and appalled. The dust jacket said it was a novel about a young heiress who is kidnapped and brainwashed and all the other stuff that would make you think it was about Patty Hearst. But it wasn't about Patty at all; it was about her, it was about Leonora. Lockhardt had changed things to make it look as if it were about Patty, but she knew he meant her. He described her as an ordinary girl, a normal girl, average in every way. So now he had finally done it. He had killed her.

Leonora put the gun to the side of her head and pulled the trigger. There was an awful noise and the gun leaped from her hand and she felt something wet on the side of her face. She had only grazed her scalp, but inside she was dead just the same.

· · ·

On the night she was committed to Agnew Mental, Leonora had forced down the beef stew her mother served for dinner and then she had gone back to her room to lie down. Almost at once she threw up into the wastebasket by her bed and then she went to the bathroom and threw up again. Back in her room she put on Phoebe Snow's *Poetry Man*. She played the album through twice, though she was not listening. She was thinking—as she had been for these last three weeks—of Lockhardt and how he had ruined everything and how someday she would let him know. But not now. Someday.

And then, as if it were somebody else doing it, she got up and got dressed and drove to the Stanford campus. She found Lockhardt's house with no trouble at all, and it was only when she had rung the doorbell that she realized she didn't know what she was going to say. But it didn't matter; somehow she would just tell him, calmly, with no tears, that he had degraded her, humiliated her, he had ruined her life.

"Yes?"

"I want to talk to you. I want to tell you something."

"Are you a student of mine? A former student?"

And then she realized that this was not Lockhardt at all, this was a much older man with a beard and glasses. The Lockhardts, it turned out, had moved to San Francisco.

Leonora got back into her car. She was frantic now, she would have to find a phone booth and get his address. She drove to Town and Country Shopping Center and found a booth, but there was no San Francisco directory. She drove to Stanford Shopping Center, and again there was no directory. Never mind. She would drive straight to the city, she would find him, he wouldn't get away from her now. She would let him know.

Traffic on 101 was heavy and it had begun to rain. Leonora passed cars that were already doing sixty. She had to get there. She had to tell him. The words were piling up in her brain, like stones, like bullets. Bullets, yes, she should have brought the gun. She should kill the bastard. A car pulled into her lane and then began slowly to brake. Leonora braked too, but not fast enough. Her car fishtailed and, with a short crunching sound, it smashed the side of a Volkswagen. She tore on ahead, though she could see in her mirror that the Volkswagen had ground to a halt, that its lights were blinking on and off. Tough. Yes, she should kill him, she thought, and she pressed her foot harder on the accelerator.

She couldn't find a parking place and so she left the car in a tow zone a block from the Jack Tarr Hotel and ran back in the rain. She found the phone booth, the directory, she opened it to the *L*'s. Lockhardt lived in North Beach. Of course he would, with all that money from *The Love Hostage*. She ran back to her car. A tow truck was backed up to it and a little bald man was kneeling down trying to attach a bar under the front bumper. "No," she shouted. "Stop it. Stop it. Stop." He stood up and looked at her, a screaming woman with her wet hair flying all around, a real crazy. "Okay, lady, okay," he said. "Okay." And then she was in her car again, tearing up Van Ness, running yellow lights, turning right on Pacific. In a few minutes she was there, at Lockhardt's blue and gray Victorian.

Leonora's head was pounding now and her back ached. She wanted to throw up, but there was nothing left to throw up. She wanted a drink. She wanted a pill. She wanted to take Lockhardt by the hair and tear the scalp off him, to expose the pink and gray brain that had written those things, that had done this to her.

She put her finger up to ring the bell, but she was

shaking so much she couldn't do it. She began to beat the doorbell with her palm and then with her fist. Still the bell made no sound. She struck the door itself, with her hand, and then with her foot, and then she leaned her entire body against it, beating the door rhythmically with her fist and then with both fists, the rhythm growing faster and faster, the blows harder and harder, until there was blood on her hands and blood on the door and she heard a voice screaming that sounded like her own.

The door opened and Lockhardt, with a book in his hand, stood there looking at the young woman whose wet hair was streaked across her face, a face distorted beyond recognition by her hysteria, and he listened to the screaming, which made no sense to him until her voice broke and he could make out the words. "I am not average," she sobbed. "I am not average. I am not average."

It was nearly a half-hour before the orderlies came and took her away.

. . .

The world had gone crazy, that's just the way it was. Leonora's mother stared at the television where for days she had been watching pictures of the 911 corpses in Guyana. They had taken poison mixed with grape Kool-Aid and in five minutes they were dead. Every one of them. And Patty Hearst had been refused parole. And so had Charles Manson. And her own Leonora in that loony bin. Leonora could have been something once. She could have been . . . but nothing came to mind. It was Lockhardt's fault, Leonora was right. It was all Lockhardt's fault. Leonora's mother turned up the volume on the TV. And now somebody had shot Mayor Moscone and that Harvey Milk. It was the way you expressed yourself today, you shot somebody.

She thought of the gun hidden in the Kleenex box and suddenly it was all clear to her. She got in the car and drove to North Beach. She had no trouble finding Lockhardt's house; she had been there three times since Leonora was taken away. She had just parked opposite the house and sat there and watched. But this time she went up the steep wooden stairs and rang the bell. She rang again and as she was about to ring a third time Lockhardt opened the door, laughing. She could hear other people laughing too; he must be having a party. Over his left shoulder, in the entrance hall, she could see a chandelier, a deep green wall, the corner of a picture. She couldn't make out what it was a picture of, but she could see that he was rich. He had everything. "Yes?" he said, and there was more laughter from that other room. "Yes?" he said again.

"Leonora," she said. "She could have been something."

And then she took the gun from her purse and leveled it at his chest. There were three loud shots and when his body slumped to the floor, Leonora's mother could see that the painting on the green wall was one of those newfangled things with little blocks of color, all different sizes, that really aren't the picture of anything.

DEPARTURES

The priest is arriving on the train. He is not really a priest, because he is only twenty-five and is still a seminarian, but he wears a Roman collar, and everyone thinks he is a priest, and he thinks of himself as a priest. It is six years since he has visited his parents in their home. They have visited him at the seminary, of course, but this is his first visit to them, and he is very anxious about it.

There is a crazy couple across the aisle, and as the train pulls into the station their anger and excitement come near to hysteria; they have just had—as they keep saying—a scrape with death. "We could have been killed," she says, her voice sharp, abused. "We've had a terrible scrape with death." She only pretends to speak to her husband; actually she is addressing the priest and the couple in front of him and the whole car. Her eyes are glassy and wild and she goes on talking with small gasps and shrieks while her husband—glassy-eyed, too, and in shock—says, "You're right, you're right," and wrestles a red plastic suitcase from the rack overhead. They are still exclaiming as they forge down the aisle, important and proud at being almost dead.

The priest waits. He does not want to be near those crazy people when he greets his parents. This will be a special moment and he wants it to be perfect. These six years have made him ill at ease in public. He cannot stand the noise, the rudeness, the urgency in voices. Emotions spill out of people, they shout in public; anger bristles everywhere, in everyone, in the street, the train station, the train. People chew gum. They belch. They push. He is revolted by the vulgarity, the nakedness of it all. In the seminary there is no emotion, no anger, no urgency—at least not visibly. Everyone keeps inside himself whatever it is he feels.

So the priest stays in his seat until the crazy people have disappeared from the car. Then he gets up, sets his face in a smile—a half-smile—and prepares to meet his parents. As he climbs down the steep iron steps, he is conscious of people on the platform looking. At him? Or just for somebody they are here to meet? Suddenly a woman shrieks and the priest turns to help her, thinking she must be hurt, thinking of Anna Karenina beneath the train wheels. But no. The woman is merely excited and the scream is only delight at seeing a boy, her son probably. "Billy," she says, "Billy baby." She hugs him, kisses him, screams again. The boy is embarrassed and the priest, embarrassed too, turns away. Mother and son, he thinks, a travesty. He has told his parents he will meet them in the waiting room, on the east side, and he joins the crowd moving toward the stairs. Ahead of him he sees another priest, about his own age, red-haired and stout. Sanity, he thinks, an oasis. But as they reach the bottom of the stairs a woman lunges at the red-haired priest, hugging him once and then again, while a man—his father, with the same red hair and fat—slaps him on the back over and over. "Father Joe," they call him, though, by their ages, he has to be their son. The woman puts her arm under Father Joe's and leans into him, her possession.

There is a disturbance now; somebody is shouting, somebody touches his arm. It is the crazy couple, even more hysterical than before, asking him something, insisting he explain to another couple what happened on the train. A little crowd is gathering and the priest, confused, turns from person to person. He is not listening, he merely wants to get away. And then suddenly he sees his mother smiling from beyond the crowd and his father behind her, his hands on her shoulders, smiling. They are a picture of order in all this chaos. The crazy woman tugs at his arm, but he pulls away from her and, moving blindly through the crowd, walks toward his mother and father. Yes, the priest thinks, I will bring order out of chaos.

His mother is beautiful, radiant, and she will not be dead for another fifteen years. She smiles and comes to meet him and he will remember her this way always. He will wake in the night remembering how she is now, what he does to her. Because as she goes to put her arms around him, as she lifts her face to kiss him, he says to her, with a smile made icy by his self-control, "I'll just kiss you on the cheek—don't touch me—and I'll shake hands with Dad, and then we'll turn and walk out of here." And he bends to kiss her on the cheek, but stops because she has pulled slightly away; she has gone white, and the look of panic on her face is not nearly so terrible as the look of drowning in her eyes.

* * *

The priest's father has been dead for five years and now the priest sits by his mother's bedside waiting for her to die. Fifteen years have passed since his train came in and he did not kiss her and she turned her face away. His mother has Parkinson's disease and the benign effects of L-Dopa have worn off, so that she is bent now and trembles violently whenever she tries to do anything for herself. She drools sometimes and sometimes she cannot control her bowels. But the priest has been told it is not Parkinson's which is killing her; it is cancer. The priest thinks a great deal about death and about the things that kill us. He is not surprised, being forty and having seen many people to their deaths, that dying is not only an agony, it is boredom. He has been waiting by her bedside for months now, an hour or two each day, and still she has not died.

His mother is unconscious much of the time. Or barely conscious; it is hard for him to tell. On the occasions when she turns to him and says something, he is astonished that very often it is something he has been thinking himself. A month before he had been remembering his father's quick death, a quick and merciful heart attack—how it had been the death his father would have chosen if he were given choices. "Your father died well," she said, and the priest leaned forward in surprise. He thought she had been unconscious. "Father?" he asked. "He died the way he would have wanted," she said. "Yes," he said, "I was thinking that." She sighed and shook her head, and a tear showed in the corner of her eye. "What?" he asked. "This is not the way I would have chosen," she said. And though he did not say them he thought the words he hated most: "self-pity." So he bit the inside of his lip and said, "Try to sleep, Mother."

Again, a week or so later, he was thinking how he had always taken from them, his mother and father; he had never given them anything. He looked at her lying there, her eyes closed, sweating, and he thought, I'll wet the washcloth and put it on her forehead. But before he could reach the washcloth she said to him, "You've always given to us. You've given us everything." And she looked at him with the drowning look.

This sort of thing has happened several times. He has begun to wonder if he causes her to think of what he is thinking: the exercise of the stronger mind on the weaker. No, it can't be that. And so he sits by her bed reading his Shakespeare—he is completing his Ph.D. in English—and sometimes he adjusts her pillows or wipes her forehead, and when she is able he talks to her. But more and more now it is a matter of waiting for the end. Her medication has been increased; even when she is not unconscious she is so heavily doped against the pain that conversation is impossible. He waits.

The priest's mother is living and the priest is waiting for her to die. He is wanting her to die now that the pain is so bad, now that he cannot bear any longer the suffering, the boredom. But she does not die.

And then finally she does die. But before she dies she wakes and talks to him one last time. He has been thinking of the train, that terrible day when he destroyed everything, when he tried to bring some order out of chaos and said "Don't touch me" and she turned away from him. He has been thinking of that all day and now she wakes and drugged, confused, looks at him and says, "You're not to worry. When the train comes in, I won't kiss you. I won't touch you." "No!" the priest cries out sharply. "Mother, no." He leans over the bed to kiss her, but as he does she turns from him, saying, "I'll be good. I promise. I'll be good." And with her dying breath, her face still turned from him, she says, "I will."

*   *   *

It is the same day. It is always the same day, except that now he remembers it differently. The priest is leaving on the train, Boston to Springfield, a three-hour trip. He is not really a priest, because he is only twenty-five and is still a seminarian, but he thinks of himself as a priest and so do his parents. His father will not die for another ten years, his mother for fifteen. They will both live to see him ordained.

The train pulls out of the station and the priest begins to read his book, Sartre's *L'existentialisme est un humanisme*. It is boring but good for him. Existentialism is good and humanism is good, and he feels that boredom is just something that goes along with the package. He reads half a page before he realizes he has no idea what he is reading. He is upset about something. What? He doesn't know. Was it getting on the train? Seeing all those people elbowing one another to get ahead, that old woman chewing gum, the man who belched? Partly that. He felt so alien, so removed from them—inhuman. All that pushing and shoving, and there are plenty of empty seats. It makes no sense.

The door between the cars opens and a middle-aged couple come in. She is carrying two shopping bags, one full of presents, wrapped in metallic papers, the other full of something the priest cannot see, because there is a sweater over the top. The man drags an enormous red suitcase, which bumps his leg at every step. It is a warm day and they are both perspiring.

"How about here?" she says, pointing to the seat directly in front of the priest, but then she sees him and says, "No, over here instead," and she backs up, bumping into her husband, who drops the suitcase and curses. "Here," she says. "Yes, this is nice. This side is better. This is fine. Sit down, Freddie. No, let me get next to the window." The man groans and says nothing, giving all his attention to getting the suitcase up into the luggage rack. "This, too," she says, giving him the bag with the presents. "No, I'll keep it at my feet," she says, and takes the bag back. Finally they are settled. The priest has watched them from where he sits, on the other side of the aisle, one seat back, and he continues to watch them. He is surprised to find the taste of acid in his mouth. He wants to spit; he doesn't know why.

Where he has felt uneasy before, he now feels anger. At himself, perhaps. He returns to his book. He is more than a seminarian, he is a Jesuit seminarian, and so he has an obligation to theology and to culture. But after another two pages he decides he does not have an obligation to Sartre and he puts the book in his briefcase. He decides to meditate. Jesuits meditate for at least an hour each day, usually on some incident, some moment, in the life of Christ, and he has never missed meditation once, not even when he lay for a week in the infirmary with a temperature of a hundred and three.

In fact, the infirmary meditation is the nearest he has come to a kind of mystical experience. He had been meditating on the Crucifixion, lying in bed with his scalding temperature, watching what was happening. He saw them drive the nails through the wrists, through the bent feet, saw them lift the heavy cross to the correct angle, until the base thudded into the stone notch that would hold it upright. There was a groan and some blood splattered onto the seamless white tunic they had stripped from him and which now lay at the base of the cross. And then there was blackness. He fell asleep, he supposed, and when he woke, his body soaked with sweat from the fever, he tried to see that white tunic beneath the cross. But he could not see it, he could see only the broad back of a soldier and he could hear the rattle of dice. Then the soldier moved and he could see the others, three of them, taking their turns with the dice, gambling for the tunic and the sandals. And when the last had thrown, one of the soldiers scooped up the dice and held them out to the priest. His hand hung there, offering the dice in his open palm, and while they all stared the priest put out his own hand and slowly, tentatively, took the dice. And then, with the small strength he could muster, he closed his fist around them.

The priest was fevered for three days more, and what he remembered after was that for those three days he held the dice in his hands. It is a meditation the priest can call back at will. He can and he does now, though he does not know why. Not because of the way it makes him feel— because feeling, he knows, has nothing to do with anything. No, he calls it back because it has something to do with *not* feeling, with the reason he is a priest in the first place.

At college his roommate had said to him one day, "Seeing as how you're a Catholic, and the best thing a Catholic can do with his life is be a priest, don't you feel obliged to be a priest?" He laughed, seeing he had struck deep. "I mean, you're smart enough, and you're moral enough—you don't screw or anything—so why not? I mean, aren't you obliged to?" The words were insignificant; it was what they did to him at that particular moment that mattered. Because he had been thinking of the priesthood and wanting, but fearing to ask for, a sign. His roommate's words seemed some kind of sign—no miraculous intervention, just the intervention of pure reason. Not a lightning bolt from heaven, he said to himself, just a slammed door. And the meditation on the dice seemed somehow a confirmation of this sign.

The priest opens his eyes. The train has been stopped for some time, new people have got on, and now it is pulling slowly away from the platform. They are near Worcester somewhere. The priest looks out the window opposite him and can see up ahead a grassy hill where three small boys are waving to the train. On the other side of the aisle the woman is rummaging through her shopping bag, totally absorbed with whatever she has in there. The man is gone—he is at the far end of the car getting a drink of water. The train pulls alongside the little boys and the priest waves to them, but they do not wave back. They throw stones, which fall short of the train—all except one, which strikes the window next to the woman with the shopping bag. It makes a sharp sound and at once there appears on the window a white spot the size of a nickel and, radiating from it, a sunburst of silver cracks. The priest sits forward prepared to do something, but there is nothing to be done. Despite the noise, like a door slamming, the woman does not seem to hear; she continues plunging her hand into the bag and bringing out things he cannot see. The other people around are either sleeping or absorbed in their reading. No one has noticed except him.

The man returns with a cup of water for his wife. She drinks it and they sit in silence looking out the window. "Was that window like that before?" he asks. "Of course," she says. And then she looks at it. "Well, I'm not sure," she says. She puts her finger on the spot of white and traces one of the cracks that radiate from it. "It looks like it's been broken," she says. "Somebody must have thrown a stone," he says, and settles back in his seat. "Well, if it happened while I was sitting here, I could have been hurt—if the glass broke," she says. "It was probably just a stone," he says. "It could have broken. I could have been hurt," she says, "if it was a bullet. It could have been . . ."

She is excited now and leans forward to the couple in

front of her. "Did you see this happen? Did you see this window get broken? Right by my head?" But they have seen nothing. She turns to the man across the aisle, to the couple in front of him, to the empty seats behind her. Nobody has seen. The conductor appears and she waves at him, calling, "Look at this, there's been an accident. Somebody broke this window right while I was sitting here."

The conductor looks at the window and at the woman and at the window again. "What?" he says. He looks at the people in front of the couple and across the aisle from them; he looks at the priest. The priest says, "A little boy threw a stone and it hit the window." "Do you see? Do you hear?" the woman says. And she turns to the priest. "Was it a stone? Was I sitting here? Right by the window?" "Yes," the priest says. "I could have been killed," the woman says to the conductor. "Do you hear what the priest said? Would a priest lie? It could have been a bullet." "Damned kids," the conductor says and moves down the aisle. "We've had a narrow escape from death, Freddie," she says, and from here to Springfield her anger and her enthusiasm grow.

The priest is sick. The chaos of life, the chaos of mind. It is all hopeless. Look at that crazy couple. The boredom of lives lived so purposelessly depresses him, sickens him. The emotion, the anger, the public displays.

The train is in Springfield but he waits until the crazy couple get off. He does not want to be near them when he meets his parents. Getting off the train, he hears a woman shriek as she descends upon her son; he sees a fat priest with red hair; he is overwhelmed by the noise, the vulgarity. And then there is a disturbance of some sort. It is the crazy couple. Her husband is tugging at the priest's arm, the woman is trying to draw him into a group that has gathered around her. "The priest saw it all," she is saying. "See that priest? He's living proof. If it weren't for that priest, we wouldn't be here now." But the priest does not hear what she says, because suddenly beyond the crowd he sees his mother, looking beautiful and composed, smiling, and behind her his father. She will not be dead for fifteen years. They will live to see him ordained, his life fulfilled.

He goes to meet them, conscious that he is in public, conscious of a small circle of order in this chaos. And as his mother opens her arms to him, he says, "I'll just kiss you on the cheek—don't touch me—then . . ." But already she has begun to turn away.

. . .

The priest is arriving on the train—New York to Boston, a five-hour trip. He has been a priest for many years and, he sometimes thinks, he is a good priest. But what is "good," he thinks. He thinks he does not know that. Sometimes he thinks he does not care. Thinking is his life now and that seems enough. Thinking and seeming. He is fifty-five and will not be dead for another fifteen years. But dying is a moment he does not care to think about.

The priest is coming back from New York, where he attended the wake of his last living relative. There is a peculiar satisfaction in that, a finality he does not fully understand but which he recognizes all the same. He would have said the burial Mass for his aunt but she died on Good Friday, which means the burial cannot take place until Monday, and so the priest is coming back to Boston, where he can be used at midnight tonight in the Easter Vigil services. And then tomorrow the Mass of the Resurrection—whoopee. He is irreverent, sometimes, in the way he thinks; it is his psyche's accommodation to absurdity, or perhaps pain, or bitterness. Anyway, he will be back in

Boston in no time, and then he will go to his room and have a good belt of Scotch, and then a couple of hours in bed to recover for the Easter Vigil.

Trains mean nothing to him anymore. He does not see the people who chew gum, who push, who carry on angrily over nothing. He does not care. That is simply how they are, that is how life is, and what can anyone do about it?

His drinking is not a problem, he thinks. It might have become one if he had not, at forty, gone for his Ph.D. in English. That has stabilized him somehow; teaching English is more human than teaching theology. He is grateful for the diversions provided by his Ph.D. He has seen too many priests hit forty and realize nothing else is ever going to happen to them, and he has seen the dodges they take—running off with the school nurse, having affairs with their students' mothers, hitting the bottle. His dodge would have been—would be—hitting the bottle. But it will not happen to him. He is careful, for now. He drinks a fifth of Scotch each week, and if he runs out before the week is over, then he goes without. Of course he does, on occasion, stop by somebody else's room and have a drink from his Scotch. But that is social drinking. That is different. He is handling his after-forty problem very well. He has no regrets, he thinks.

The train pulls into the station and he pushes his way to the front of the car. He is eager to get off and get home. He does not hear the woman who shrieks with pleasure as she descends upon her teenage son. He does not notice the demonstrations of anger and frustration and delight. He does not even smell the rank odor of cigarette butts and urine. He just keeps his eyes cast down and makes his way through the waiting room to the cab stand. Leave the dead to bury the dead, he used to think as he left these depressing public places, but now he does not think about them at all. He is a priest who has left the world to itself, truly.

He is home in his little room and he pours himself a Scotch and drinks it. He showers and stands in front of the long mirror examining the evidence of too much food, too much drink. He will have to cut down. He puts on his yellow pajamas and sets the clock. He has four hours before he must put on vestments for the Easter liturgy; and so he stretches out on the bed and closes his eyes, ready for sleep. But the trip to New York and the aunt's wake and the trip back to Boston swim through his mind and he cannot sleep. He feels good, and he feels guilty for feeling good. The boredom is over, those long hours on trains, the unpleasantness of all those strangers at the wake. Over is good, he thinks. Finality is good. But what is good? Well, he *feels* good and that's something.

The priest wakes from a nightmare. His head aches and he has trouble getting his breath. He is shivering. What was he dreaming? He cannot remember. He is late. He hurries through his shower, shaves, dresses, his mind going back and back to the dream. But always it eludes him. Perhaps it was the soldier dream again. He no longer meditates, but often in his sleep he sees the soldier's back and hears the rattle of dice. The soldier shifts position and the priest sees the others, three of them, taking their turns with the dice. Finally, as always, the last one scoops up the dice and hands them to the priest, who takes them and closes his fist on them and when he looks down—this is the new part, the awful part—he sees that blood is oozing from between his fingers. And then he wakes up. The old meditation, which for years gave him some kind of abstract comfort, has turned to dream and to nightmare. But it was not the soldier dream tonight, it was . . . And again the dream eludes him.

The priest is vested now, saying a brief prayer before leading the procession to the rear of the chapel. The vigil is a long and complicated ritual and in his mind he ticks off the major sections. There is the striking of the new fire—a tricky business, because all the lights are out and you have to fumble around with the flint device. Then the blessing of the new fire, the blessing of the Easter candle, the solemn procession. The singing will be tough, because he has a weak voice. The readings. Then the blessing of the baptismal water . . . Death by drowning, he thinks, and for a second his mind veers to *The Waste Land,* but then he comes back to the vigil. The baptism of the baby—he must check the baby's name before that part of the ceremony—and then the litany and finally, at midnight, Mass. Fire and water. Burning and drowning. Light in the darkness. The water that gives rebirth. It is a symbolism so ancient, so basic, that it must guarantee a reality, he thinks.

And so the ceremony has begun and the priest stands in the vestibule surrounded by the entire community. The lights have been extinguished in the chapel and now the light over the door goes out and they are plunged into complete blackness. They are waiting, all of them, for him to strike flint against flint and start that spark which will be the light shining in the darkness. The flint grates and grates again, and just as he has begun to think he will never get it to work right, there is a flicker and a dot of light and then a flame. The flame catches in the little pot of wax and by its light the priest begins the blessing of the new fire.

"The Lord be with you," he says. And the community responds, "And with your spirit." He breathes easy, because the rest of the prayer he knows by heart. He stares into the fire, reciting the blessing. "Let us pray. O God, through Your Son Jesus Christ, You bestowed the light of Your glory upon the faithful. Sanctify . . ."

But then, in the fire, he recognizes his nightmare. He sees the soldier's back and hears the rattle of dice; the soldier moves and the priest sees not the three other soldiers but his mother; her drowning face is turned away from him and her hand is held out. In her hand are those dice— bloody, eyeless.

"Sanctify . . ." the priest says once more, and now it is time to raise his hand in blessing, but for the moment he cannot, and he continues to stare into the fire. "Sanctify . . ." he says again, staring and staring, still unable to bless, unable to go on or turn away.

"Sanctify . . ."

The word echoes in the darkness and the light flickers until with his bare hands the priest reaches forward and puts the fire out.

ANSWERED PRAYERS

1
. . .

When he died, he was ready for it, more or less.

He was pulling out of a side street, thinking about God, when he realized the car approaching on his left was not going to stop, not even slow down. It struck him broadside, doing sixty. He felt his own car rise in the air, twisting, and he caught a glimpse of the astounded face of the other driver, and he said to himself, Now I'm dead. Then he heard a tearing sound as his car fishtailed into a chain link fence, and he said to himself, Well, I mustn't be dead after all. What luck. But he was dead by the time the ambulance came.

His name was Donovan Enright and he had been a

Jesuit priest, with a lot of Jesuit ideas. They buried him with a guitar Mass and an upbeat homily.

2

.   .   .

Donovan Enright had nothing in common with Gene Sullivan, the man who killed him, except that they both were Catholics and they both were forty-five.

Donovan had been a Jesuit for twenty-seven years and a priest for fourteen of those years. He had kept his vows as well as any priest and better than most. Which is to say, as Donovan himself had said more than once, "You can spend a little money and still be poor, and you can do what you want to and still be obedient, but you can't fuck around and still be chaste." That was one of his Jesuit ideas. Mostly, Donovan kept his vows by keeping to himself. He had trouble making friends, and most of the Jesuits he knew best were too intellectual for that sort of thing anyhow. And besides, life was a lot less complicated if you stuck to your own room and just thought. Once, during the religion craze of the sixties, he put some of his ideas on paper and published a book about the Death-of-God theologians. He didn't think much of them and the Jesuits didn't think much of his book. So he went back to teaching theology and sitting in his room with his ideas until one night Gene Sullivan killed him and his life was different forever.

Gene Sullivan's only vows were his marriage vows and he kept them as well as most men. In his late thirties he had had a steady mistress, but when he turned forty he decided to play the field. He was a cop and so had opportunities. He hung out with his police buddies at the Up Front Café, which featured a topless hostess and a girl who wore white boots and half a bikini. The girl in the boots was Needa Mann and she worked out on a little platform way in the back, snapping her fingers and moving around in time to the music. Gene had made it with Needa, as all the other cops had before him, and she was good. Even just watching her snap her fingers and roll that sweet butt could take his mind off home. At home was his wife, Jayne, who always had big pink rollers in her hair, and his daughter Sheree, and his son Kevin. After night duty the guys all got together at the Up Front and had a few beers. One night Gene left the bar early and cruised the Combat Zone until he found a girl he had picked up twice before on lewd and lascivious. She saw he was out of uniform and knew what the deal was, so she got into the car and gave it to him parked in the A&P delivery dock. He went back to the Up Front then, feeling shitty, and had a couple belts and then a couple more. He was mad, at himself, at his whole goddam life. There was no way out of anything. Life was a trap.

He was thinking this while he drove home to Jayne and, preoccupied, did not stop, did not even slow down, until his car struck Father Donovan Enright's car. His life was different after that.

3
. . .

"We've been on this subject for a week now, Father, and I'm still not sure what you hold. Are you saying that there *is,* or there is *not,* life after death?"

Father Enright was still alive at the time, so he pushed his glasses back on his nose and leaned into the question.

"That's a rather simplistic formulation of the problem, wouldn't you say?"

"Yes, it is. Can you answer, please?"

Students turned around to get a look at the questioner.

"Simplistically, yes, there *is* life after death. But immediately the question arises, what do you mean by life? Or, for that matter, by death? What would be wrong, say, about the rather Protestant notion that we live after death in the memories of those we have known, of those who care about us? Just as, for example, Lincoln or Gandhi or even Jesus live in our memories."

"But aren't most people, after a short time, not remembered at all? What about *their* eternal life?"

Father Enright pounced. "Ah, you see? Democracy of the spirit. The life of the soul, Mr. ah—Mr. Smith, is it?— the life of the soul is rooted in mystery. It has no room for democracy. We did not elect God, we are not all equal. Why should not each of us, therefore, enjoy an eternity proper to himself? A life perfectly fitted to the life we led on earth?"

And then he went off onto his other favorite ideas and everyone relaxed because none of that would be covered in the final exam.

4

. . .

Gene Sullivan took one look at the body in the car and knew it was all over for that poor bastard. He checked the area, the skid marks, the position of the two cars. By the time police arrived he had a plausible story ready, one that would stand up in court, so long as nobody measured the skids, etc. The guy must have been drinking, he said. He came shooting out of that side street like a bat out of hell, never stopped at the sign, must have been drunk, he said. By the time the ambulance came, it was clear the guy was dead.

Somebody found his wallet and it turned out he was a

priest. That was good in a way. No lawsuit. No family. But, Christ, a priest!

Chico Mulligan drove Gene home and had a drink with him.

"Don't worry," Mulligan said. "I'll fill out the report myself. Maybe he was drinking, maybe he was speeding. I'll take care of it. We're buddies, right? You'd do the same for me, right? All right, so don't worry!"

After Mulligan left, Gene poured himself a tumbler of Four Roses. Then he woke Jayne and told her how he was almost killed, how the other guy was dead. She kissed him and hugged him and then poured him another drink.

"Come on," she said, "come on, baby," and she led him off to the bedroom, where for a whole bunch of reasons he couldn't do anything. "Forget about what happened," she said, her hand busy beneath the sheet. "Put him out of your mind."

Finally he fell asleep and then she fell asleep. But even in his dreams, Gene kept seeing the dead priest's face.

For Donovan Enright, the dead priest, it was the first of many unusual nights.

5

· · ·

So this was it, Donovan thought, I'm gonna be summoned every goddam time! At first he couldn't figure it out, but after the third time he realized it fitted perfectly with everything he had thought about an ironic God.

It went this way. The cop would be doing his stupid police work and minding his own business and then all of a sudden he'd stop and think of that priest he killed, and once he thought of him he couldn't get him out of his mind. That was Donovan's signal. He had to drop everything and live locked in that mind until the cop forgot about him. Tough shit that, for Donovan, life might be going along nice and peaceful, his ideas on heaven and hell and eternity clicking by with smoothness and precision; as soon as Gene thought of him—whammo—it was all over.

Some eternity. Some joke. It had been going on for months now and Donovan was beginning to get fed up.

6

. . .

"As to the question of eternal reward—or, as you have just formulated it: is there a heaven and a hell?—I would say yes, there is a heaven and a hell. God rewards us by giving us whatever it is we have always wanted."

He had paused then, and even the dullest of them had looked up. Father Enright was known to be peculiar, but surely he was not actually proposing a pie-in-the-sky heaven.

"That is to say, if you have put yourself first in all things, then that is what you'll get: you'll spend eternity looking *in*, contemplating yourself. But if, on the other hand, you have lived for other people—for God, if you wish—then you will spend eternity looking *out*. Looking out at what, I would not care to say."

They had continued to stare up at him, perhaps imagining him dead. A vein throbbed in his temple and he had looked severely at the thirty-some expectant faces as he said, "Those who are determined to be damned will find, I think, that their peculiar prayers are answered."

The next week he was killed in that fishy car crash.

7

. . .

At first, Donovan hadn't minded much. It wasn't like being dead at all, this summons to somebody else's life.

"Come on, baby," Jayne had said, and then she had taken her husband to bed and fooled around with him. Donovan hadn't gone along at first, in and out of Gene's mind as he was, but as Gene got excited, the thought of the priest returned more and more strongly to his mind, and so Donovan had no choice. Poor, obedient, and chaste, Donovan wrestled in that bed, his heart racing and his body pumping wildly right up to the moment of release. He gasped along with Gene, flopped over on his side, and waited till his heart slowed down. Donovan was just about to submerge beneath a tidal wave of self-disgust, when Gene suddenly forgot about him and fell asleep. Donovan was finished with and went back to his old thinking.

Gene made love to his wife often now, and sometime during the event invariably called up that damned priest. After a few of these times, Donovan came to realize that this was his afterlife, it was God's will, and he began to surrender to it. Who was he, after all, to pick a quarrel with God? The sex was terrific, and the complexity of the emotions that went along with sex was a revelation. Sometimes while Donovan writhed in what he continued to think of as the act of love, he would shudder with a surge of undiluted hatred, and then he thrust hard and his chest expanded with the feel of punishing and he thought, Good, good. And sometimes when they were having dinner, he would look at the cop's daughter—because Gene would look—and think of the things he could do to her, how it would feel, how it would teach her what was what. Donovan even found himself once—when Gene was shaving and his son came in to take a shower—he found himself thinking about the kid. My God, the kid? But Gene cut himself then, maybe deliberately, and so the priest went straight out of his thoughts.

That kind of variety kept Donovan in a continual state of wonder. Life had never seemed like that. No such thoughts had ever crossed his mind while he was alive. Or had they? No. He had never even made friends with Jesuits, let alone with women. It was too much of a risk. He had wondered once, in his late twenties, if maybe he was queer. He had wondered for quite a while, and had even thought of seeing a shrink, but decided finally that if your car was up on blocks, it didn't really matter whether it was manual shift or automatic drive. And then in his early thirties he decided he wasn't queer anyhow. And now all this: the wife, the daughter, even the son.

A few months passed and the summonses became more frequent. Donovan was beginning to get fed up.

8
. . .

The summonses became more frequent and more boring: while Gene was on duty in the prowl car, while he sat swilling beer in the Up Front, while he—God help us—sat on the toilet fiddling with himself. Every few hours his mind would slip from whatever he was doing and sure enough that damned priest would be back. Gene became jumpy and irritable, not just at home, but everywhere. He was not sleeping nights. He was never relaxed. He could not keep the face of that dead priest out of his mind.

Gene couldn't figure out why. He had killed guys before, two of them. Some kid in a stolen car had pulled a gun on him and he had had to shoot it out. And he had killed another guy, a Puerto Rican who had gone nuts and was holding his own kids hostage. Gene had killed both of them and never thought about it for a minute. But this priest here, he couldn't get out of his head.

And then one night when he and Chico Mulligan were on duty in the wagon, they got a 10-13 to West Roxbury. It turned out not to be a 10-13 at all, just a couple of kids who broke the window of a liquor store. One of them they'd picked up before, Jesus Sanchez, a punchy bastard who was always looking for real trouble and someday would find it. Sanchez had a bottle of Canadian Club in his hand, and as the two policemen came at him, he broke it off at the neck and made a lunge at Mulligan's face. Mulligan used his leather sap and decked Sanchez with one tremendous blow to the side of his head. "Humane," Mulligan said, letting Sanchez lie there while they frisked the other kid and then hustled him into the wagon. Then they got Sanchez by the hands and feet and tossed him into the wagon too. But as Mulligan was about to slam the door, Sanchez kicked out with a pointed shoe and caught Mulligan flat in the chest.

In seconds the two cops were inside the wagon. Gene held Sanchez from behind while Mulligan worked him over. Sanchez went limp and Gene dropped him to the floor, but Mulligan was not done. He kicked the body up against the wall and then worked up and down, getting him in the shins, the knees, the crotch, the chest, using his sap on the back of the head.

"Christ," Gene said, "you're gonna kill him," but Mulligan didn't stop. And then there was a siren from a squad car, and then another, and Gene pulled Mulligan off Sanchez.

"Resisting arrest," Mulligan said. "You saw him."

"Right," Gene said.

But before they brought him into the station, Mulligan took the precaution of slipping some uppers into Sanchez's pocket.

Gene filled out the report the way Mulligan wanted; it was what you had to do for a buddy.

But the next day when Sanchez died without ever regaining consciousness, Gene thought of the priest he had killed—he couldn't tell why—and from then on the priest was constantly in his mind.

Donovan had to relive the beating the two cops had given Sanchez. But now it was he who held the struggling Sanchez. And it was he who—along with Chico now—swung his foot at the shins, the knees, the defenseless crotch. After a while Donovan realized he almost liked the feeling as his foot crunched against the yielding flesh. Yes, he liked it.

It was then that Donovan began to wonder if he had gone to heaven or to hell.

9

.   .   .

In an "Afterword" to his book on the Death-of-God theologians, Father Enright had recorded various unconnected thoughts about the mysterious nature of sin and punishment.

"The God they say is dead is actually the democratic God of their own fabrication. The true God, the God of justice and of irony, lives forever."

"Sin is behovely. Therefore, irony is behovely. How else explain Julian of Norwich, among other wonders."

"It would seem that God allows pride and arrogance to go unpunished. He does not. It is only that some sins cannot be punished except by other sins. Thus the man of pride is often allowed to slip into sins of the flesh. Sometimes we cannot find ourselves until we are wholly lost."

A lot of crazy ideas, his fellow Jesuits said. They felt he did too much thinking, alone in that room.

10
. . .

The day after Sanchez died, two things happened.

The first was that Gene Sullivan went to Confession. He didn't know why he went, and he didn't want to go, but he ended up inside the confessional anyhow. It was as if he'd been dragged there, with no power to resist. He told the priest that awhile back he had been in an accident. He had had a few drinks, he said, and maybe he was a little under the influence because he really hadn't seen the other driver and, anyways, he had killed him. The priest asked a lot of questions, like was there a family left behind and all that, and Gene said no, no, nothing like that, and after a while the priest gave him absolution. But as soon as he came out of the confessional, it started in all over again. He hadn't admitted that the guy he killed was a priest or that Chico Mulligan had filed a false report saying the priest had been drinking, so he figured the Confession was no good and the Sacrament wouldn't take. He was right back where he started. He stood for a minute on the church steps wondering if he should go back and tell the rest. *"O bone Jesu, exaudi me."* He looked around to see who was talking, but nobody was there. Jesus, he said to himself, and all the way down to the station he played rock music really loud, but he kept on hearing that smooth voice saying, *"Exaudi me."*

The second thing happened down at the station. Chico Mulligan came up to him and said he had to talk, so they got into Mulligan's car and drove out toward Brookline.

"I gotta get this card for my wife's anniversary, see. We'll go to this place where Reilly's girl works, The House of Cards, wait'll you get a look at her tits. Out to here."

Gene's mind was still on Confession; the voice he heard had to be that dead priest's voice. The thought made all his teeth ache.

"Tits out to here," Mulligan was saying.

Disgusting, Gene thought. And to Mulligan he said, "Look, Chico, I got a lot on my mind. I don't give two shits for Reilly's girl's tits." He was trying to get that priest out of his head.

"Hey, that's a song, practically," Chico said. And in a deep bass, to the tune of "On Top of Old Smokey," he roared out, "He don't give two shi-its, for Reilly's girl's tits, de da da da *da* dum, de *da* da da dum."

"Come on, for Chrissake, Chico! Don't you ever get serious?"

"I been serious." Mulligan gave him a sideways smile. "I was serious the night you killed the priest. Yeah, I been serious. I was serious all right when I filled out that report. 'Tread marks, none. Alcohol consumption . . .' "

"All right! All right! Forget I said anything. Just forget it."

"I can forget, Gene old buddy. Old Chico, he can forget. By the way, how's *your* memory?" he said, as he parked the car. He slammed the door on Gene's answer.

In The House of Cards, Mulligan was feeding Reilly's girl a whole string of double-meaning gags, so Gene pretended he was looking at cards. He picked one up and opened it as if he were reading, but he could hear the sex in Mulligan's voice, and he shook his head. Goddam pig, he thought, and took a quick look at Mulligan and the poor girl. "Better a millstone be put around his neck," Gene said aloud, and the girl looked over at him, smiling, and then back to Mulligan.

"Geez, I like your tits," Mulligan said. "I mean, your cards. Your cards, I mean."

Mulligan and Reilly's girl laughed it up then, but Gene left The House of Cards and sat waiting in the car. He couldn't figure out what was the matter with him. It must be the Confession, he figured.

In a minute Mulligan came out of the store, laughing, but when he got in the car he was all business. "It's about Sanchez," he said.

The kid they brought in with Sanchez had got word out to some smartass reporter that Sanchez had been beaten to death. There was going to be an investigation. Gene Sullivan would have to testify.

"What about Sanchez?" Gene said.

"He was resisting arrest, you remember that. He was crazy with drugs, so I had to subdue him. I hit him twice. You remember that."

"Yeah, I know that."

"I remember how it was with your priest. You remember how it was with my spic. Right?"

"Right."

"Right. So just don't change your mind when the heat gets on."

They drove back to the station, Chico Mulligan singing his song about Reilly's girl's tits, Gene Sullivan wondering why he kept thinking the things he was thinking.

His mind was no longer his own. He began to wonder if he was losing it.

11
. . .

The smartass reporter had really started something with his story about the death of Jesus Sanchez. There were riots in Roxbury, minor ones, but they got a lot of press coverage. The hotshot social scientists started coming out of the woodwork, writing editorials in the Sunday paper and demanding police reform. Chico Mulligan was investigated for police brutality and, although a lot of stuff surfaced about his beating kids and fags and spics, there was no hard-core proof. But then every other day there were stories about graft and police rip-offs and insurance to small businesses, until finally the word came down from city hall to pick a couple of guys and kick them off the force. With plenty of publicity. So Chico Mulligan was on his way out and Gene Sullivan was under investigation.

Jayne was crying every day now at breakfast, just sitting there sucking on her bad teeth. And his own kids looked at him like he was shit. Gene spent a lot of time at the Up Front and a lot of time just driving through the dark streets. Donovan Enright had become his constant companion. The dead priest's thoughts filtered through Gene's mind so that Gene never knew anymore what he was thinking and what was being thought for him.

As for Donovan, he was tired as hell of all this and was going to end it even if it killed him.

Gene had resisted the temptation to go to Confession again and this time tell everything. And he took desperate steps to maintain control over his own mind. He had thought about it plenty and finally came to the conclusion that the only way to get a priest out of your head is by a lot of drinking and screwing and taking chances. So when he got off duty, he'd go straight to the Up Front. After a few drinks, he'd cruise around in his car and pick up a hooker, twenty minutes with her and then back again to the Up Front. Then he'd drive the turnpike, getting the speed up to eighty, ninety, seeing how close he could come to an abutment before he'd chicken and swing the car back onto the lane. He was crazy, he knew it, but he would do anything to get away from that voice inside his head.

Finally he'd go home, drunk, and collapse in bed next to Jayne who lay staring at the ceiling. Next morning she'd be crying at breakfast. Gene didn't know where it would end.

Donovan knew.

12
. . .

"O Lord, we commend to You the soul of Your servant, Donovan, that, having departed from this world, he may live with You. And by the grace of Your merciful love, wash away the sins that in human frailty he has committed in the conduct of his life. Through Christ our Lord. Amen."

Then the singing:

> *Day of wrath! O day of mourning!*
> *See fulfilled the prophets' warning,*
> *Heav'n and earth in ashes burning!*

And a whole lot more. It was a nice service, really, if you got rid of those damned guitars. Donovan was looking forward to it, again.

13
. . .

On the last night of his life, Gene got the word that he would be temporarily relieved of duty until the investigation on him was complete. Seems they had turned up some hard evidence about payoffs and falsified reports, and they were looking into his involvement with the numbers. No sweat, Gene said, and took off for the Up Front.

Needa Mann was strolling to the music, snapping her long fingers, when he came in and took a seat up close to the stage. He had a beer. After that he had some John Jamison and a beer for a chaser. Needa twitched her butt at him and he gave her what he hoped was a hungry look.

"When you're hot, you're hot," somebody said to him. It was Reilly, drinking a beer.

"He who lives by the sword, dies by the sword," Gene said to Reilly, and thought, Jesus, this is really it, this is really the end.

Gene and Reilly had a few more beers.

Donovan let the liquor settle in, waiting for his chance.

After a while Gene went to take a leak. There was nobody in the men's room and Gene stood in front of the mirror for a long time, looking at his face. Then he took out his pistol and put the barrel in his mouth. He looked at himself like that and after a minute turned in profile to see another view. He could blow his head off. All he'd have to do was just release the safety and press the trigger. Then it would be all over—the life, the wife, the whole shitty deal.

The door slammed open and he pulled the barrel out of his mouth quickly.

"Thought you fell in," Reilly said.

"Up yours, Reilly." Gene put the pistol into his holster and went to get another drink. But Donovan had had enough of the Up Front and was eager to get on with life. And so Gene ordered the drink but didn't wait long enough to drink it. Before he knew where he was, or why he was there, he was in his car heading for home.

It was after midnight and he sat in the kitchen waiting for somebody to keep him from what he was going to do. He had placed the pistol on the table in front of him. He wouldn't use it . . . unless. He got a bottle of Four Roses and a soup bowl full of ice. He filled a tumbler with ice and booze and drank it slowly. After a long while, he got up and walked down the hall to the bedroom. Jayne was asleep, the big pink rollers in her hair. He went back to the kitchen and waited. He fiddled with the pistol for a while and then poured another tumbler of Four Roses.

He was dozing, his head on his arms, when he heard Kevin saying, "You drunken pig."

Gene looked up and saw his son, so young, so defenseless. He wanted to protect him.

"You are," Kevin said. "A drunken pig."

Gene stood up woozily. He put his arms around the boy, hugging him, trying to find the words to tell him how things were. "You don't know," he said, slobbering.

Kevin pushed with both hands against his father's chest and Gene was flung against the wall. His head snapped back hard and, sobered a little, he slipped to a fighting crouch ready to take the boy on. But Kevin had left, and Gene stood with fists clenched, facing an empty doorway. He picked up the pistol, turned it over in his hand a couple of times, and jammed it into his holster. Then he was slamming the door hard and the car wheels were churning gravel on the driveway and he was out of it, once and for all.

He was not thinking now, it was too late for thought. He was in the car, driving down to the Combat Zone. But he passed through the zone without even checking out the girls. At the Hancock Building he stopped the car long enough to toss his belt and holster into the backseat and slip his pistol into the door clip next to the driver's seat. Then he drove directly to the meat rack. He'd pick one up, a butch one, and he'd beat the shit out of him. He'd dump him in the A&P lot. It didn't matter why. He'd do it.

He cruised slowly around the block twice, slowing down to check out what was for sale. He stopped at a big muscular kid with white pants and shaggy blond hair. Gene blinked the caution lights and the kid ambled over to the car.

"Hi, guy," he said, putting his head in the window.

"Get in," Gene said.

The boy tipped his head from side to side, checking Gene's face and build. "Hmmm," he said.

"Get in."

"Regular or special?"

"Regular."

"How much?"

"Ten."

"Ten?" He pulled away from the window.

"All right, twenty."

The boy got in then, and they drove around making small talk about the weather.

"What's your name?" Gene said.

The boy laughed. "Smith," he said. "What's yours?"

"Jones."

"What else? Say, tiger, can we get this over with? I don't feel like driving around all night."

Gene pulled into a side street, and down an alley, and finally he parked behind an apartment building. He tried to work up some anger at this fag he was going to beat the shit out of. He tried to recall why he had to do this, but Donovan was lodged firmly in his mind, and Gene could feel nothing. But he had to. He had to mangle this kid. That was why he had come down here. That was why he had picked the kid up, why . . .

And then suddenly, with the force of revelation, he knew exactly why he was here. Leaning his head against the steering wheel, he gave way to long racking sobs that shook his entire body. He cried as if he intended never to stop.

After a long while Gene felt a hand move on his back and shoulder. "That's okay, that's okay," he heard the boy saying. "Coming out is hard at first."

"You don't know," he said. "You don't know what any of this is like."

The boy only tipped his head to one side and pursed his lips.

Gene felt the boy's hand move on his leg. He shook off the hand and drew a long, deep breath. Then, his mind on nothing but the dead priest, Gene backed out of the parking place and pulled out of the alley and eventually onto the turnpike. The car accelerated to fifty, then sixty.

The boy next to Gene gave him an anxious look and moved away from him. "You're driving crazy," he said. "I want to get out."

Gene took the pistol from the door clip and pointed it at the boy's head. "I'm a cop," he said, "and if you touch that door handle, they'll have to pick you up with blotting paper. You're coming with me." With the boy beside him cringing against the door, Gene lowered the pistol and pressed harder on the accelerator.

He drove straight into the deep night, of one mind about life and death, as the speedometer hit eighty, ninety. The abutment loomed before them and Gene kept his hands firmly on the wheel. There was a roaring sound inside his head and then, for the life of him, he could not recall anything about why he was doing this. But at the very moment of impact, the priest's astounded face flew up suddenly before his own, and he heard someone say, "Now I'm dead," and could not tell if the voice was his own or the priest's.

And what happens now? Gene thought, or maybe it was Donovan.

14

• • •

Miraculously, the boy survived. He was thrown free of the
wreckage and was found unconscious in the middle of the
speed lane. He had two broken arms and a slight concus-
sion, but no permanent injuries.

He was out of the hospital and back on the job in only
a few months, but it took him just about forever to get that
damned cop out of his mind.

DESIRES

ROMAN ORDINARY

His Holiness Pope Paul VI is an ordinary saint. All day long he does what he has to do, and at night he dances.

First thing in the morning, after meditation and Mass, he has a little orange juice and a sweet roll with butter. Some days coffee. Some not. It depends on what Romagnoli brings. And then His Holiness goes to the toilet, but not very much. Afterward, he makes his bed.

Then it's business, business, business without a letup. Cardinals are in and out all day: Vatican finances, the pill, a paternity suit against some bishop. Cardinals Bagnio and Konig present in outline their report on Opus Dei, a suspect lay order in Spain; it turns out that Opus Dei is allied with the right wing of the curia and it turns out too that its influence in Spain, and even in Italy, is benign. Not only tolerable, but benign. *Floreat Opus Dei.* A decision must be made on the secret archives of the Vatican Library. And what about that Benedictine nun who said Mass in Chicago? Is His Holiness thinking of—how can we put it—retirement? Perhaps when he is eighty? No? Pilgrims are lined up and waiting for the papal blessing, a sea of believers awash in their saris and double knits and platform shoes. So much ugliness and hope. Did Christ have all of this in mind? The thought flickers for a second through the papal consciousness, but His Holiness extinguishes it with the single bat of an eyelash. He smiles distantly. He speaks a few words of welcome in German, in French, in Greek, in English. A cardinal whispers to him and then he welcomes the Indians and the Slavs. People dear to our heart. All one in the love of our Lord and Savior Jesus Christ. Some damn fool snaps a picture even though cameras are forbidden. After a while they all let His Holiness go and he trails his long white robes behind him to the papal apartment. Time for a lie-down.

The papal apartment consists of a sitting room, a bedroom, and a bath. The sitting room has four little chairs, designed to be uncomfortable, and a big desk where His Holiness sits during private audiences; lots of faded tapestries cover the walls. The bedroom is huge, with a glistening parquet floor and almost no furniture. A wooden bed of no special design stands over near the windows; at its head there is a small armoire which holds the pope's robes, and next to that a bureau for his socks and underwear and hankies. On the opposite wall stands the great armoire to which Pope Paul VI alone has the key.

His Holiness lies down on the narrow bed, but the quiet doesn't last long. That little priest Romagnoli is banging around in the sitting room, laying out the tea. Cold tongue of lamb, three caramels, a piping cup of Constant Comment. His Holiness bolts the lamb tongue because he is always famished in midafternoon. Then he sits back and tucks a caramel into the side of his jaw and sucks at his tea. This is his private time, with the shoes kicked off and the old feet up, just enjoying his caramels and tea. Life is good. When he was younger, he used to meditate on the transitoriness of all things mortal during this teatime, but now that he is in his late seventies, he makes his mind a blank. Nothing. Nothing is happening.

His fifteen minutes are up now and the little priesty-poo is chapping at the door, ostensibly to take away the tray, but really to edge His Holiness into the next round of duties.

Delegations are waiting from Russia, from Persepolis, from Houston. The mistress of a South American dictator demands, for the twentieth time, a private interview. Cardinal Wright is waiting to talk about Joan of Arc and about election procedures for choosing the next pope. A monsignor from *L'Osservatore Romano* is owed a private word because of his ringing defense of the personal lives of two curial members—kinky, both of them; and perhaps after the private word, His Holiness could pose for a quick photograph? Investments in obsolescent housing must be liquidated, now, while prices are still adequate. A bishop is waiting, a cardinal has a special report, three monsignori have brought money in dollars. Can Henry Ford remarry? Can President Ford? His Holiness attends to all these matters, his frail yellow hands pressed hard against the white breviary he carries everywhere, his mind only occasionally wandering to the night and to the great armoire in his bedroom.

Finally the work is done and he is free. He goes to his private chapel and prays, sometimes for only twenty minutes, sometimes for an hour. He goes out of himself during this time, looking back wistfully at his own kneeling figure, or looking down from the Stations of the Cross high on the gilded wall, or—more and more lately—looking off to nothing, nothing at all.

Dinner is laid in the papal sitting room: a large bowl of granola, an apple or an orange or some exotic fruit in season, a single glass of wine. It is ten o'clock by now and Rome is beginning to come fully alive. His Holiness toasts the city and its twenty layers of civilization, roof built upon ruined roof, bone upon bone.

Everything is in the process of decay. While the number of Catholics has continued to increase, the number of priests has dropped: last year from 344,342 to 339,635. The Vatican deficit is about $6.4 million. The Americans don't give a damn. What to do? His Holiness shakes his head slowly, wisely, from side to side. Again he raises his glass to Rome, to the Via Veneto with its Ferraris and movie stars and Anita Ekberg, and beneath it all to the catacombs with their still unexplored chambers of whitened bones.

After dinner it is canasta time, or blackjack, or honeymoon bridge, whichever Romagnoli prefers. Monsignori, bishops, cardinals, indeed all ecclesiastical Rome dreams of someday playing canasta with His Holiness, but those dreams will never be realized. His Holiness plays only with Romagnoli, the young priest who brings his meals and tidies up around the place. A Sicilian, hot-tempered, Romagnoli plays to win and usually does.

At eleven that Dominican, private confessor to the pope, appears at the door; at eleven-thirty, his soul washed clean, His Holiness takes to his bath so that by twelve he will be fully prepared.

It is a few minutes to twelve now and almost time. His Holiness puts on his pajamas of some rough cloth, immaculately white. The trousers balloon out shapelessly, but they are tied at the ankles with thin brown ribbons. The top slips over his head and is gathered at the waist by a brown sash. The sleeves are wide and loose. His white slippers turn up at the toe like a medieval jester's. He is almost ready. He goes quickly to the small bureau near the head of the bed and, reaching far back into the top drawer, he withdraws a large square of white cloth embroidered with brown. In the center of the cloth there is a circle of leather which will protect his skull from the knife blade. He folds the cloth carefully and then places it on his head, the circle of leather directly on the crown. He tucks the folds of cloth back from his face, arranging it like an Arab burnoose, and then binds the headdress firmly into position with a brown silk circlet. In the mirror he adjusts the silk cord across his forehead and smooths out any wrinkles in the cloth. Is this some sort of Jewish rite? Is this some compromise with Mohammed? The embroidery along the edge of the white cloth could tell us something, surely, but we cannot examine it closely enough because there is no time.

The bells of Rome have begun to proclaim midnight. While they toll on and on, His Holiness walks to the great armoire and turns the little key smoothly in the lock. The carved double doors swing open.

His Holiness genuflects and then stands with his palms together in the attitude of prayer. But he is not praying. He is marveling yet again at his wonderful bones.

The armoire before which he stands contains a tier of thirteen shelves, each of which, at the mere touch of the papal finger, slides out to provide ready access to its contents. Pope Paul VI presses one of the lower shelves where his large bones lie on a ground of purple silk; gently, soundlessly, it moves toward him until it touches his folded hands, and then it stops. Spread out there before him in perfect order are his femur, his tibia, his fibula. Next to them lie clavicle, humerus, radius, ulna; in the shelf above, the metacarpal and the phalanges. Light from the ceiling casts a violet shadow on the bones and they glow almost with a life, with a soul, of their own. He presses gently on the shelf above this one and out slides a display of his corpus, his tarsus, his patellae. And then the special shelf, the one with his skull intact, the bones very nearly articulate. His Holiness runs his fingers lightly over the forehead and his pale hand tingles. The eye sockets are smooth round holes, yellowing at the edges; he pokes his thumb into that strange aperture, no eye there, no vile jelly left. The pope catches his breath. This is how it will be, later, when at last he lies dead: his bones will wait in some dark vault for something, for anything. And yet they lie here now, put away out of sight, out of use, while he goes on each day living the life of an ordinary saint. His breath comes quicker, lighter. He presses the shelf above, and the shelf above that, and then rapidly, one after another, all the shelves but the top one, each with its cargo of white and glistening bones. *His* bones.

The double doors stand open, the shelves of the armoire expose their treasure to the empty room and to the pope, who has begun to back away. Facing the huge armoire, he bows deeply and then, thumb and middle finger pressed together, he raises his arms out from his sides until he stands cruciform. It is a flamenco dance? He extends one leg to the side and brings it forward suddenly in a kind of crouch, spins on his forward foot in a sweeping circle, and then repeats the motion with his other leg. No, it is not flamenco. He is dancing slowly, ritually, like a harem dancer, like some small Persian boy trained to do this and this alone. His headdress flutters behind him and the full sleeves flow and dip to the fluid motions of his arms. He is losing himself, his eyes have taken on a distant look, as if he sees beyond this room and these bones he honors with his dancing.

Now the pope approaches the armoire in a formal hesitation step. He bows low for several measures and then he presses the topmost shelf, which slides toward him bearing the long curved sword with which he must dance. Tenderly he lifts the sword in his two hands and holds it up, like a presentation, before the armoire. And then he moves to the other side of the room and makes his presentation, and then to the next and the next. In the center of the room he stops. His head is bowed. He summons his considerable powers of concentration and then, decisively, he places the sword squarely on the crown of his head, the curved blade poised on the circular leather patch, the tip hanging to the left side of his head, the handle to the right. He adjusts the sword for balance, but it continues to teeter. A fraction of an inch to the left and then it rests motionless. His Holiness takes a tentative step or two. Perfect. The blade whispers against the leather but remains in balance.

His Holiness is smiling as his body moves about the room. The small feet glide soundlessly on the parquet floor. The muscles in his back and belly ripple like water. As his frail torso lurches forward and back, his buttocks respond and his thighs follow through. He dances slowly and with grace. In their exposed shelves, his bones are radiant. He dances on and on, though the bells of Rome have struck one o'clock and then two. It seems he must stop now, surely he must, he has danced so long. But he continues.

And now he kneels, the blade on his head dipping from right to left. Slowly, so slowly he can feel the blood pulsing in his thigh and temple, slowly he sits back upon his heels. He slides somehow to his hip and then his buttock until, incredibly, he is lying on the floor at full length, but with his head erect and the sword in calm and easy balance across his crown. Ecstatically, all the muscles of his body ripple, for he has completed this impossible thing. On their shelves his bones clatter. It is done.

With a sudden twist of his entire body, His Holiness is on his feet once more, free now of the most exacting part of his dance; the rest is sheer jubilation. He dances gladly, arms swinging out and away from his body, legs twining and untwining as he moves in arcs and arabesques undreamed of. On and on he goes, though the minutes slip by, though the clocks strike again and again. His flesh ripples and flows. The garments that surround his flesh seem to float free of it. There is nothing beneath those garments but water or air. No flesh is there, surely.

Pope Paul VI's bones have rested in the armoire for how long now, attended nightly by this ritual dance. And now the flesh is gone as well. Yet His Holiness dances on, his eyes glazed and all-seeing, his body and bones reduced to pure spirit.

Later, unfleshed, His Holiness will kneel at the window to watch dawn break and later still he will crawl to bed for an exhausted hour of sleep before the rest of his world awakes and Romagnoli comes to announce time for meditation and Mass. He will take up again his make-believe life of interviews and reports and decisions, pretending. But now it is the dance that matters.

The dance winds on faster and faster and the sword too moves with an independent life. His Holiness twists endlessly clockwise and the sword, its curved silver blade glimmering in the light of the bones, twists counterclockwise, faster and faster as His Holiness Pope Paul VI, that ordinary saint, dances out of his flesh and bones, and dances.

WITNESS

Morgan Childs was a born manager. By the age of forty she had managed her way into a marriage, a son, a divorce, and a tenured professorship of statistics at a major West Coast university. She had a reputation as a model California woman—that is, one who could independently raise a child, chair a university department, conduct a love affair with flamboyance and with style. She managed always to initiate the affairs and, when the time seemed right to her, to terminate them. Afterwards she always kept her lovers as friends.

Morgan Childs and Jamie O'Hara met for the first time when he was tending bar at a faculty Christmas party. He was only twenty-six and looked even younger, but Morgan asked him if he liked women who were forty and he said yes. And what else? Well, he had been a semi-narian for three years, he was now a graduate student in psychology, and, desperate for money, he tended bar at faculty parties. Like now. She said that was nice because she needed a drink and there was a high degree of probability she would need another tomorrow afternoon at three. And so they met the next afternoon at her place, and they had another drink, and then they went to bed. The affair lasted from Christmas till Easter. It was early in Lent—Lent bothered him, he said—that Jamie first told Morgan he wanted to break it off.

"You're jumpy," he said. "And you make me jumpy."

"I'm usually the one who ends these things," Morgan said.

"And then there's my wife. And the kid."

"I'm not sure I'm ready yet to break it off."

"Not to mention *your* kid."

"There's the matter of my wrists, after all."

"And most of all my religion. It's all right for a Jew, maybe, but I can't do it during Lent."

"I'm not a Jew."

"Catholics can't. At least I can't."

"That is, not a practicing Jew."

"Well, it's over. Period."

And so at Easter Jamie left her and went back to his religion and his wife and the kid. Morgan had no family to go back to; her divorced husband was off somewhere in Israel plotting against Arabs and her son Julian had left three years earlier for Choate and came home now only for summer break. Of course, even if she had a family to turn to, she wouldn't have. What could a family tell her about this sickness, this disgrace? What could anyone? Because, by the end of their affair, Morgan bore upon her elegant Jewish wrists the bloody wounds of her new and inexplicable condition.

•   •   •

The pain in her wrists had begun a full month before the wounds actually appeared. She had just finished her afternoon class in applied multivariate analysis, and she was driving back to her apartment to meet Jamie for a quick one before he would rush off to his family and she would rush off to the ballet. She stopped for the long light at Page Mill Road and, though she had resolved to quit, she said what the hell and reached for a cigarette. She was thinking about Jamie and his hard little behind and about not being late for him when, with no warning at all, the cigarettes flew from her hands and a pain shot through her left wrist so hot that tears sprang from her eyes, and her hand flapped wildly in the air as if caught in some terrible machine. She screamed once, a high light sound, and pitched forward onto the steering wheel, her right hand clutching her left wrist, her face twisted in agony. And then the pain struck her right wrist as well.

She was completely conscious. She was aware of her foot pressed hard on the brake and she was aware that the light must have changed because cars were speeding by her on both sides, and behind her someone was honking a horn. She was aware of all this, but for a long minute she could do nothing about it. It was as if only the pain existed; it spread from her wrists up her arms and out, to fill her whole body; it possessed her. Her own existence had ceased altogether.

And then some man was shouting at her, rapping at the window. "Are you all right?" she heard him say. And then there were two men, rapping, staring in at her. "I'm all right now," she said. "I can manage." Somehow she pushed herself back in the seat and with her dead hands clinging to the wheel she steered the car forward until she was able to get it into the right lane and finally to pull to the curb, where she turned off the ignition and waited to pass out. But nothing happened. The pain in her wrists—incredibly—was gone. Her head was aching, her breath was coming in short heavy gasps, but there was no pain at all in her wrists.

Had she imagined it? No. There was no mark of any kind, no cut, no burn. She could believe—she could prove—it had never happened, except for the certain evidence: the cigarettes had flown from her hands and were scattered on the seat and on the floor. And that pain. That pain was its own evidence.

She shook her head. She was forty and getting a little crazy. She was working too hard. What she needed was Jamie O'Hara's good hard body. She drove home fast and, without a word about what had happened, she took him straight to bed.

• • •

A week later it happened again. This time she was alone in her office. She had been preparing a lecture on Hotelling's T^2 statistic when it struck: the same sudden pain, the same wild flapping of the hands, the scream, the tears, and then nothing, nothing at all. Afterward, when she came to herself, she discovered that she had snapped her pencil in half and scattered her notes and papers everywhere. Her desk was a shambles.

It had happened in the car while driving, it had happened now in her office; it could have happened anywhere, even in the middle of a lecture. A lecture. She imagined those hundred and twenty faces turned up to her in disbelief as she broke off talking about the organization of data and began to scream and flap her hands in the air and roll her head back and forth with the terrible pain. No, she couldn't risk having that happen. Something had to be done, and now.

She strode from her office and off to the parking lot and from there directly to the emergency room of the university hospital.

"You'll have to be more specific," the doctor said, frowning.

"It's happened twice," Morgan said. "Once at the intersection of Page Mill and El Camino Real about a week ago. Exactly a week ago. And again today in my office, perhaps half an hour ago. Or thirty-five minutes." He looked at her in a funny way, but said nothing. "The pain is hot and sharp. Like a needle, a heated needle, something larger than a size-seven knitting needle. And it strikes here. Exactly here."

The doctor took her left wrist in his hands and pressed the spot she indicated. And then her right wrist. "But it doesn't hurt now?"

"No."

"Here?"

"No."

"How about here?"

"I showed you where it was. You've moved a full inch away."

He sat back in his chair and looked at her. "There's no sign of anything. No sign of an injury. No sign. Do you use your hands a lot?" He gave her that funny look again.

She checked the name tag on his lapel. Underhill. She didn't know any Underhill. And yet he looked at her as if she should, as if they were in collusion about something.

"Manual labor, I mean? Gardening? Some sport?" He gave her half a smile.

"I use them," she said. "But not in a way that would explain that pain."

"All right," he said, "very good," and stood up as if he had settled everything. "We'll have you X-rayed and see what turns up."

She was already at the door when he said, "You really don't remember me, do you?"

"Underhill?" she said. "How do I know you?"

"Think."

"Doctor, I have no time for games."

"Not underwater games? In honor of Saint Patrick?"

At once it came back to her. Every year the Callahans held a Saint Patrick's Day party to which they invited absolutely everybody they knew. It discharged their entertainment obligations for the entire year and it broke up the spring semester perfectly, and just about everybody went. The Callahans had a heated pool and last year, late in the party, Morgan had gone swimming in the buff with a nice young man with remarkable ability to perform sexually even underwater. That nice young man, she realized now, was Dr. Underhill.

"I'm sorry," Morgan said. "I *am* sorry." She smiled at him as if he were Jamie. He winked; or, it seemed to her that he winked. "I think at a moment like this, the socially correct thing to do is go straight on to X-rays."

The X-rays, however, showed nothing except the finely articulated bones of her elegant wrists. Dr. Underhill studied the X-rays carefully, examined her wrists once more, and returned again to the X-rays. It was a fluke, he said, it would probably never happen again. She could relax. It was mysterious but not meaningful. And, he assured her with that half-smile, he looked forward to seeing her again at the pool.

• • •

It might happen again and it might not. But Morgan taught statistics and she knew the odds and she was determined that if it did happen again, it would not happen in public. And so the next Friday she took the precaution of canceling her class and staying home in her apartment. She would get through this thing, if she must, by herself.

She drew the curtains and put *Parsifal* on the stereo and settled in for a pleasant day of total distraction. But for the first time those long thin opening strains failed to draw her along with them; instead she caught herself lightly rubbing her left wrist with her right index finger. And then her right wrist with her left index finger. She found she could locate the precise point of . . . of what? Of entry, she was thinking, as if she had been violated somehow. Raped. And yet there wasn't a mark, not even a shadow. She held her wrists up to the light as if she expected somehow to see into them, to see something lodged there, something growing that would eventually burst through the skin. But nothing was there, and meanwhile the overture to *Parsifal* had ended and Act One had begun and she hadn't paid any attention at all.

She snapped off the stereo and picked up the new Harold Robbins. She didn't bother with the titles; they were all the same, trash. But trash gave her what she looked for in fiction; human psychology at its most uncomplicated level. The good and the bad. The right and the wrong. Problems of human behavior presented, jazzed up, resolved. Robbins was all very satisfying, with just enough sex thrown in to make it read easily. But this one didn't hold her and after four or five pages, four and a half to be exact, she realized she hadn't been reading at all. She had been mentally counting her pulse beats, her attention given over to the soft throbbing in her wrist. "Damn," she said aloud. "This is hopeless."

She phoned the psychology department to leave a message for Jamie, but when the secretary answered, Morgan thought better of it and hung up. She must get through this day alone. She must reassure herself that the pain was a fluke and that young Dr. Underhill—that underwater surprise—was indeed right, that she had nothing to worry about. And so she baked a streusel swirl cake for her son Julian. She would package it and mail it off to him at Choate. Very maternal, that. And then she repotted three philodendrons, the only kind of plant she had any luck with. And then she took a long bath. But still the day dragged on. It was only two o'clock. She wondered if Jamie would phone. No. He'd drop by her office or phone her there, but he wouldn't guess she'd be at home. She turned on the television and looked at "One Life to Live." It was so slow, so boring. How did women watch these things? The heroism it must take to be a housewife. She flipped the channels; it was the same sort of crap on all of them. On "The Doctors" there was an intern who looked very much like Jamie. He was trying to get out of a relationship with Lois or Helen or somebody. He had no reason, he just wanted out. Yes, very much like Jamie. "The Doctors" ended and "Another World" came on. God, how could she get through this? She sat in the darkened room staring at the flickering images on the television, the blond heads, the perfect teeth, all those confused faces, but she thought only of the pain she was expecting. She was waiting for it, yes, she wanted it over and done with. She flicked off the television set and closed her eyes. "When it comes, I'll be ready," she said.

But she was not ready. At exactly 3:18—she had just opened her eyes to check the time—the pain struck so hot and sharp that she was lifted from her chair, writhing, shaking, until she slipped to the floor on her knees with the agony of it. She lay there for almost an hour, gasping, with terrible lights shooting behind her eyes.

It stopped finally and she sat up and examined her wrists; there was a small bruise the size of a nickel on the inside of each. Dizzy, drunk almost, she staggered to the telephone and called the psychology department to leave a message for Jamie.

"He's right here," the secretary said, covering the mouthpiece but not covering it well enough. Morgan heard her say, "It's her," and giggle.

When Jamie took the phone, Morgan asked him in her new jumpy way—as he called it—to come over at once. He had to get home, he said, he had to baby-sit while the wife went to the Stations, he had to . . .

"Come now or don't ever come again, you bastard," she said, and he heard something in her voice that he had never heard there before. He was at her apartment in less than twenty minutes.

They sat in silence, neither of them knowing what to say. A cup of tea was set before Jamie; Morgan sipped brandy from an outsized snifter. After a while she put the snifter down and began, slowly, to tell him everything: she recited the previous incidents in meticulous detail, she described the pain, she showed him the bruises on her wrists. When she finished, she sat back and waited for his reaction. And Jamie, the fool, looked her straight in the face and laughed.

"In the seminary we'd have said you were a stigmatic. You know, like Theresa Neumann."

"A what?"

"A stigmatic. One of those saints that have the wounds of the nails in their hands." Morgan merely stared at him, expressionless. "From when they nailed Christ to the cross, you know—"

"I know what a stigmatic is," she said. "I'm trying to—"

But Jamie was enjoying this and would not be stopped. "—I mean, he's got these wounds here and here, and some saints get them too. It's all very mystical. Maybe you're one of the chosen."

Morgan struck him then. She slapped him hard on the side of his face and, as he sat there astounded, she slapped him twice more. Then she leaned back in her chair and reached for the brandy snifter. "I'm dead serious," she said, "and you're playing the Catholic fool."

There was silence between them for a long time.

"We're going to have to break this off," he said finally.

"Because I slapped you?" She was still angry, but holding it in.

"Because it's against my religion. I should be with my wife at the Stations, not screwing you in the middle of a Friday afternoon. It's wrong, Morgan, it's just wrong."

"I might point out that you are not screwing me and what on earth station are you talking about?"

"The Stations," he said. "The Stations of the Cross. During Lent—"

"I don't want to know," she said, furious all over again. "I detest that religion. I detest Catholics and everything they stand for. It's sick, what they say and do. It's demeaning. It's dehumanizing. Catholicism is not the opiate of the people, it's the lobotomy of the people. It's, it's . . ." and her rushing voice cracked and she lowered her head and began to cry quietly.

Jamie rose and placed his hands on her shoulders. She threw her arms around his waist and hugged him to her. "Come to bed," she said. "I want you." He sighed deeply and continued to stroke her hair. "I need you," she said, something he had never heard her say before. "What?" he asked. She pulled away from him and smiled crookedly. "Yes," she said. "I need you. I'm that desperate, that I'd say it." Jamie laughed softly, but she ignored him. She began to knead his small behind and as he leaned into her, she pressed her face against him. She unbuckled his belt. "Like a whore," she said, smiling up into his face, but it was unlike any smile he had ever seen. Frightened and strangely aroused, he lifted her from the chair and carried her into the bedroom.

.   .   .

Morgan resolved never to see Jamie O'Hara again. She would do what she had always done when she broke up an affair; start a new one. And so on Sunday, though she had intended to skip the Callahans' annual Saint Patrick's Day party, she went, and almost the first person she ran into was the one she was looking for, young Dr. Underhill from the emergency room.

"Well, look who," Morgan said. "We meet once a year, it seems."

"Except for medical emergencies," he said. "How's that wrist?"

"Well, it doesn't keep me from using my hands."

He gave her that funny look of his and she was ready with her own.

"Let me get you a drink," he said.

He was gone for a while and Morgan took in the pool and the garden and the people milling about, the same old people telling the same old stories. It was depressing. "Dissidents? Dissidents?" she heard someone say. "I can tell you about dissidents. I've been a prisoner of conscience for most of my life." It was worse than depressing. Morgan's forced high spirits were deserting her rapidly. She thought she might just leave. Yes, she would leave. But by then Underhill was back with her drink.

"To our annual swim," he said, clinking his glass to hers. But as she drank, he said to her, pointing, "That's a mean-looking bruise you've got there. Let me take a look at it."

"No," she said, and pulled away. "Don't touch that."

Her voice was high and sharp and people looked around at them. "Sorry," she said. "I mean it's just a silly bruise. It doesn't even hurt."

"Your other wrist has one too. What have you been doing, pounding nails with your hands?"

Her face twisted then. "Why don't you go for a long swim," she said. "Why don't you go drown." She handed him her glass and left him and the party and went home.

She poured herself a glass of brandy and drank it pacing up and down the living room, through the bedrooms, in and out the bath. She tried to make her mind a blank, to obliterate by the power of her will Jamie and Underhill and those damned bruises on her wrists. She finished the brandy and poured another; she sat down to write a long chatty letter to Julian. "Dear Julian," she wrote. "I'm sorry as hell you've decided not to come home for Easter, but you can be sure we'll make your summer break a very special one. I miss you, Juli, more than I ever have." And then, though she had intended to write about campus gossip, something he always enjoyed, she found herself writing, "I have this pain in my wrists that is worrying me sick." She stopped writing and stared at the paper. She stared at her wrists. She was becoming obsessed. She was half-mad. She poured herself another drink, then tore up the paper and drove back to the Callahans' party.

She got herself a drink and moped around the edges of conversation groups trying to look absorbed. The party was reaching its final phase; people were passing a cigarette from hand to hand, inhaling deeply, seriously, and then exhaling the thin silver smoke slowly, waiting. The crowd had thinned and was thinning even more. There were four people in the pool, all in bathing suits, and as Morgan watched they came out and toweled themselves off by the bug lights, laughing, shivering at the sudden cool.

"We've got to stop meeting this way," Dr. Underhill said from behind her. "You've come back?"

"To say I'm sorry. And to get a drink." She held out her empty glass.

"I'll get you a drink."

"Do."

He came back with the drink. "I get a second chance?" he asked. "Shall we start over?"

"Let's."

"Okay. That's a mean-looking bruise on your wrist. I've been thinking about it."

"Not that. Forget about the damned bruise."

He smiled that half-smile, but said nothing.

"You're quite a swimmer, I recall," she said.

"I'm best underwater," he said.

"Promises, promises." She downed her drink and held out the empty glass.

"Are you *trying* to get drunk?"

"One more. And then we'll stroll to the dark end of the pool and in no time it'll be our time to swim." But she had two more drinks before the party had thinned enough for nude swimming.

Three or four people were stretched out in lawn chairs, smoking good Colombian and half sleeping, half listening to the reggae that still came from somewhere inside the house. Morgan and Underhill were alone in a corner of the pool.

"Jesus, look at you," Underhill said, and he slid his hands from her waist up to her breasts and around behind her shoulders. "You've got a fantastic body."

"Enjoy it," she said.

"I will," he said. "Slowly and thoroughly and, believe me, this time you'll remember who I am."

She laughed and led him on, playing with him the

way she knew men liked. They were all the same and she was an expert at this sort of thing. And so when he entered her, she was more than ready, and she threw back her head until it rested on the tile border of the pool. Her hands lay lightly on his shoulders.

He was caressing her, supporting her. And then she became aware that, even as he was thrusting slowly back and forth, his hands had moved from her buttocks to her breasts and then to her arms. He ran his hands to her elbows, to her wrists. In the dark, feeling his way surely and finally, he found the bruises on her wrists and began to press them with his thumbs.

"Is this how you like it?" he whispered to her. "Is this how he does it?"

The water churned slowly as he continued to thrust, but Morgan was aware only of the strange feeling at her wrists.

"No," she said, but he only pressed harder. "Do you like it?" he said. "Do you want it?" as the dull hard pain he was causing pressed into her wrists and into her consciousness. She raised her head from the tile, fully aware now of what he was doing, and desperate to stop him. She shouted something unintelligible and tried to strike him but he held her hands tight in his own. She sank her teeth, hard, into his shoulder and as he pulled away from her she tore her wrists free. She bore down on him, struggling, and with a kind of preternatural strength, drove him to the bottom of the pool. Her hands were at his throat and as she pressed down on him she kicked against rising in the water. She felt his head strike the cement at the bottom of the pool. He was struggling fiercely, pushing against her, his arms and legs flailing the water, but he was unable to break free. And then, suddenly, he stopped fighting her because her hands came loose from his throat and his body rose, sodden, to the surface of the water. He stood, gasping and choking, and braced himself against the side of the pool. He spit out some water, gagged, and threw up. He tried to call for help but no sound came out. He looked down at Morgan who was lying on the surface of the water, facedown, her long hair spread in an aureole about her head. He grasped her shoulder and turned her over on her back. Her eyes were open. Jesus, what a mess, he thought. He called for help, but whoever it was in the lawn chairs at the other end of the pool was beyond hearing.

He dragged her out of the pool and kneaded her abdomen with his fists until water shot in small jets from her mouth, and she threw up, and finally came conscious. They lay sprawled side by side in silence, the only sound was their labored breathing. After a long time he propped himself up on an elbow and studied her face.

"You play rough," he said.

"I'm crazy," she said.

"Who'd have guessed it. A little S & M underwater. I can dig it. I like it. But you could have warned me."

"Take me home? Please?"

"I'm up for it."

"Please."

He took her home. When she woke the next morning her back and her behind were covered with welts. A man's leather belt lay on the floor next to the bed and pieces of her torn clothes were scattered everywhere. The silk cord from her robe was still knotted around the bedpost. Morgan turned her head toward the wall and pulled her knees to her chest and began to shake soundlessly.

.   .   .

So this is madness, she had thought then, this is what it means to be insane. And she lay in bed the entire day, reduced to a kind of stupor. She would never leave this room again. She would die here.

But by Tuesday morning she decided that this was insanity indeed, to lie in bed and let one awful night overwhelm you. She got out of bed determined to take control of her life and put it in definitive order. She resolved to stop smoking and drinking. She did the laundry. She cleaned the bathroom. She went to her office and caught up on paperwork. When Jamie phoned and left a message, she did not phone back. Her life was her own, by God, and she was going to keep it that way.

That afternoon—Tuesday—she lectured on design of experiments; Wednesday afternoon she lectured on discrete censored data; Wednesday evening she broke down and had a pack of cigarettes and several drinks; Thursday she saw the psychiatrist.

"I was lecturing on psychological data and factor analysis, Dr. Sloss, when suddenly it occurred to me that perhaps I'm imagining this pain in my wrists."

"Imagined pain can be real pain."

"It is real, that's what I mean. But I wonder if thinking about it, being obsessed by it, could bring it on."

Dr. Sloss leaned forward in his chair and fixed her with his milky blue eyes. "It's none the less real for being obsessive."

"I mean it's not a physical thing. There's nothing here you can point to and say, 'It's a broken bone, it's a strained tendon, it's arthritis.' It's nothing like that. So if it's not physiological, it must be psychological. There has to be some logical explanation. *I* must be the cause of it. Do you see?"

"You would make a very good psychiatrist. You see things very clearly."

"But if I am the cause, then what do I do about it? How do I stop myself imagining it?"

"You go so far and then you stop."

"What do you mean?"

"Well, it's obvious, isn't it? Just think for a moment."

"Think of what? There are facts, hard data, to consider here. Facts have explanations. Facts can be dealt with, even psychological facts. Fact: *I* must be causing this. Response: how do I stop it?"

Dr. Sloss smiled at her and said nothing.

"Well?"

"I am amused at how you've passed over the obvious. If you are the cause, as you say, of these bizarre pains in your wrists, if you are imagining these pains, as you say, the question is not how do you stop it, but why are you imagining it. Don't you agree? The question is why do you want this pain? Why do you need it?"

Morgan's face went red.

"When you can tell yourself why you need it, you may find it disappears like magic."

Morgan stood up and moved toward the door.

"Tell me about your childhood," he began, but she was already out of the room. He shrugged and buzzed his secretary. "Make an appointment for Mrs. Childs a week from today. She'll want to see me again."

Back in her office Morgan found a note from Jamie saying he had broken off with her; he had to go back to his family and his religion: it was all over. "So go," she wrote on the bottom of his note and walked over to the psychology building to leave it in his box. But there at the door were Jamie and the department secretary talking and smiling, leaning into one another in that way Morgan knew so well. "Another fact," she said to nobody, and crumpled up the note. Underhill and Sloss and Jamie O'Hara. And her wrists, of course, she mustn't forget her wrists. All facts. If she could say why she needed any of them, maybe they would *all* disappear like magic.

She returned to her office and told the secretary to cancel her Friday class.

"But there is no class," the woman said. "It's Good Friday."

"Good Friday," Morgan said. "I'd forgotten."

"Well, of course, it's your holy days too, isn't it."

"No. Yes."

"Well, anyhow, Catholic or Jew, it's a day off, right? And we can all thank God for that."

Morgan went home to wait.

•　　•　　•

Magic. There were no probabilities to magic. Given enough skill, every trick was guaranteed. And here was the solution to her problem: sleight of hand. On Friday morning she drove to Dalton's and bought three books on magic and for the next several hours she practiced making a large linen handkerchief assume the shape of a duck, a rabbit, a mule. She practiced making a nickel disappear, making it turn into four nickels, making it come out of her ear. She was clumsy and none of the tricks really worked, but the practice was time-consuming and required intense concentration and, for a while at least, she was able to put the idea of the pain out of her mind. She had a long lunch in town and returned home at quarter of two, determined to practice her magic and outwit that damned pain. There was something right, something mathematically perfect, about using sleight of hand—gross magic—to outwit this thing. She was convinced that if she could keep her mind completely distracted at three o'clock, she would escape the pain this time, and forever. Like magic.

But precisely at 2:00, as she twisted her handkerchief into a perfect rabbit, the pain struck and her hands seemed to be wrenched free of her wrists. She threw back her head and waited and waited. When finally she looked down she was not prepared for what she saw. A small trickle of blood flowed from the wrist into the palm of each hand and the foolish handkerchief was spattered with bright crimson spots. "No," she screamed. "No." But the blood continued to trickle from her wrists into her palms and onto that handkerchief. She stared, sullen, at the awful sight. "It means nothing," she said. "Nothing at all." She crumpled the handkerchief and flung it from her. But the blood fell, a tiny drop at a time, to the dull gold carpet at her feet.

•   •   •

Morgan dreamed that night that Jamie O'Hara had tied her to a cross and was hammering nails into her wrists. "You're a stigmatic," he said. "You're the real thing." And he hammered and hammered. "You've been chosen, Morgan. You have no choice in the matter." She woke up with a terrible thirst and a headache and a pain in her side. "God damn you, Jamie O'Hara," she said. "God damn you to hell."

But in the afternoon she went to the reference library and looked up *stigmata* in all the encyclopedias. "Stigmata are the signs of the wounds Jesus sustained in his crucifixion or the pain associated with such wounds that have appeared in some of his followers who have had ecstatic experiences." She raced down the page, reading carelessly, jumbling facts and dates. The first well-known stigmatic is Saint Francis of Assisi (about 1181–1226) . . . Saint Catherine of Siena . . . Saint Teresa of Ávila . . . no two cases are alike . . . modern examples are Teresa Neumann (1898–1962) and Padre Pio (1887–1969), who were examined medically and shown to have signs of wounds . . . no evident reason to suppose that the production of the stigmata surpasses the power of nature . . . the most common feature is the stigmatic's consciousness of being identified with the suffering of Christ.

She read all the encyclopedia accounts, short and repetitious, and she checked the card files under *stigmata, the preternatural, the supernatural.* She found a book by Biot called *The Enigma of the Stigmata* and read it through, going back and back again to passages that seemed to describe her own case. But when the library closed and Morgan went home, what she took with her was one sentence: "There is no evident reason to suppose that the production of the stigmata surpasses the power of nature."

• • •

Dr. Aaronson had won a Nobel Prize for his work in hematology when he was still a very young professor in Munich. But pressured by hospital authorities to engage in genetic research on what they referred to as "expendable" patients—some Jews but mostly just idiots—he fled Germany in thirty-five and ever since then had taught and studied in the university hospital. Morgan had chosen him as her last resort. He was old, and she wanted somebody old, and he was certainly not a fool. If Aaronson couldn't help her, then nobody could. She had phoned him the night before and said she realized he no longer saw patients, she realized he had only emeritus affiliation with the med center, but would he see her as a service to science? She had a problem that so far defied rational explanation, it defied pure reason. "For you, my dear, no. For pure reason, yes. Come at eight tomorrow morning."

And so on Monday morning at eight, Morgan sat in his office waiting for his verdict. Dr. Aaronson had examined her and found nothing; he questioned her about specifics of time and place and the variability of the pain's intensity. He sat back for a long while, looking at her.

He had deep-set brown eyes and heavy white eyebrows that half concealed them. His heavy German accent made everything he said seem portentous, but something in the timbre of his voice made him sound bemused.

"Are you a hysteric, Miss Childs? No, I think."

"Rarely," she said. "No."

"No, I thought not." He sat in silence again, and then he said, "From the phenomena you describe, from the absence of any physical or psychological explanation, I have to conclude that, unless new data present themselves, that you have been how shall I put it 'blessed' with the stigmata. I am very glad I agreed to see you. You are familiar with the stigmata? Yes?"

"I am a Jew, Doctor. I do not believe in God. I hate religion of any kind because of the superstition it breeds and the harm it does to believers."

"Yes?"

"I have no aspirations to sanctity or indeed to any kind of singularity arising from belief in God, especially belief in a Catholic God."

"Yes?"

"Furthermore I am what people call promiscuous. Very promiscuous. I find it hard to imagine that the Supreme Power has singled me out as the right person to carry around with her the wounds of Jesus Christ. No. There is another explanation, a scientific one, and that's what I've come to you to get."

"Of course, of course," Dr. Aaronson said. "And we'll get that. Together. So come to me on Friday and let me study the phenomena as they occur." He smiled and put his hands together as if in prayer.

"Not if you insist that this is the stigmata."

"Does calling it one thing or another change the nature of it? It is what it is."

"But what *is* it?"

"Let us call it a scientific curiosity," he said. "Come on Friday."

On Friday Morgan spent the day with Dr. Aaronson

and he observed the phenomena as they occurred and he concluded that, call it what she would, it was remarkably like the stigmata.

"But I am a Jew," she said.

"So am I," he said. "This must be studied. This must be watched. This is very exciting."

"Exciting for you, perhaps. For me it is terrifying. I feel as if I am haunted, possessed, as if there's some other life in me."

"Ah," he said. "That may well be," and he raised his bushy eyebrows and smiled.

•　　•　　•

The next Friday there was no pain and no mark upon her wrists, but the Friday after that the wounds bled once again. Morgan was prepared now for any eventuality. She had bought several new dresses—Friday dresses, she considered them—with long sleeves ending in ruffles which half concealed her hands. Around her wrists she wore her tennis sweatbands to catch any blood that might flow. She was ready. She would ask help now from no one. She was not going to be somebody's terrified lover and she was not going to be a spiritual guinea pig either. She was in this alone.

The time she used to spend on pleasure—on Jamie and on all the others—she now spent on books. In class she was lecturing on tests of significance and, though the material was highly complex, her presentation was lucid. Theorem, proof, example. Theorem, proof, example. Her mind clicked over like a computer these days and her tongue found all the right words. They were good lectures: everything accounted for and explained.

But she had not accounted for or explained the marks on her wrists. Sometimes she bled, sometimes she had only the pain, sometimes there was nothing. She could no longer predict what would happen, or even when. She had bled once on a Thursday evening, and then again early Friday morning; on another Friday she had torn off the sweatbands to staunch the flow of blood only to find there was no blood at all, only a small whitish star on her flesh.

Dr. Aaronson phoned. "Has it happened again?" he asked. "The scientific curiosity? Yes? Both the wounds and the bleeding?"

"Sometimes both, sometimes just the pain."

"It's as I said. The stigmata."

And he called back the next week and the week after that. "It's the stigmata," he said. "Why don't you let me study this? You could make a gift to science, yes? Let me study you."

"I'm studying it," she said. "I'm making progress."

But in fact she was making very little progress. She had studied the bone, nerve, blood system of the hand and arm. She had studied normal and abnormal cuts, wounds, abscesses. She had studied medical oddities of every kind. In desperation she had even statistically calculated the probability of having a disease never before isolated in medical history. The probability was infinitesimal.

Unwillingly, therefore, but determined to resolve this contradiction in logic, she took from the library everything she could find on the subject of stigmata. Most of what she found was hagiography, accounts by blindly credulous old priests of saints—women usually—who went for years without a bite of food, who prayed day and night, in and out of ecstasy, and whose principal reason for existing seemed to be to pour out buckets of blood periodically from wounds in their hands or feet or sometimes both. Any account was like every other: heroic sanctity right from the cradle was rewarded in later life by these bloody testimonials to God's favor. Terrific.

She went back to Biot's *Enigma of the Stigmata,* which

she had raced through months ago when all of this began. She liked the title. An enigma was a puzzle, a problem, a set of facts. Enigmas could be resolved, understood, and finally dismissed. But what she found in the book failed to resolve the enigma; rather, it compounded the problem. Case histories succeeded each other in a dizzying display of unreason, impossibility, contradiction. But Biot's approach was scientific, suggesting possible origins of the stigmata in hysteria, neurosis, even psychosis. He gave his closest attention to modern cases where there was verifiable medical evidence. He was detached, concerned with hard facts. But what struck Morgan in every one of Biot's accounts—and how was it possible she had missed this before?—was his insistence that no stigmatic had ever claimed personal sanctity.

So she could be . . . it was possible . . . granting, of course, that there is a God.

No. There was another, an obvious alternative. She was simply mad, like those poor lunatics in the saint books she had been reading. Yes, she would rather be mad.

And, it struck her, she really was mad. She began to peer at herself in mirrors and store windows to see if she could catch herself off-guard, to see if she could see what others saw. She still looked like a well-kept forty-year-old woman who had her life perfectly in control, but she knew otherwise. Her life was out of control, her mind was out of control. And then the pain came, and sometimes the blood, and she would hug her wrists to her chest, cradling the madness against her. Like Lucia, she thought, or like some poor crazy witch they hanged in Salem. It was not God or the devil, it was simply madness.

She had nightmares every night now and they carried over sometimes into the day. She found herself one morning in her office staring at a piece of graph paper, mentally filling in the little squares to form the image of a body stretched upon a cross. Suppose these wounds, these mental lapses, were from some spirit—God, say—how would you fight it? or them? She took a pen and began filling in every other square of the graph paper, but in her mind she was in a singles bar, picking up a man, any man at all, taking him home, taking home two at a time. She lay in bed, letting them use her, letting them invent new ways to grind pleasure out of her body and at the moment of climax she shouted, This is for you, how do you like it, I'll beat you at this yet.

She ground her teeth and continued to fill in the squares. She could call Underhill and have him bring his sex toys, tie her to the bed. But of course it was stupid to think of using sex against God. Only Christians and Jews thought sex had a moral dimension. Certainly God didn't.

She caught herself then, thinking dangerously.

She kept a bottle of vodka in the bottom drawer of her desk for emergencies such as this and she poured herself a stiff shot. If there is a God, she thought, why is he doing this to me?

She was still filling in squares when a student knocked and came in and saw Professor Childs drinking vodka and filling in little squares on graph paper.

"I'm sorry to come here out of office hours," the girl said, "but I've got a class, like, during your hours."

"I've been thinking about God," Morgan said. "What do you think about God?"

"Well, I really don't know," the girl said. "I'm not really that much of a Jesus freak."

Morgan laughed and said, "Jesus freak; that's good."

"What I came in for, actually, was to ask if I can take your course for a pass instead of a grade? Even though it's like past the deadline to let you know? I mean, I wonder if you'd let me?"

"Do you think God would let you?"

"Actually, I don't know. I think so though."

"Well, then, you may. I want to be at least as generous as God."

"Oh thanks. I mean, really. You've saved my life," the girl said, backing to the door. And outside she said to her boyfriend who was waiting for her, "You wouldn't believe it, Childs is drunk out of her mind," and they went off together to smoke a joint and celebrate the good life.

•   •   •

Morgan was drinking herself to sleep these days and sleeping badly at night and then drinking a little more to get herself going in the morning. "I can't help it," she said to the mirror, "this is just what mad people do." And she looked at her wrists, bruised today, a sign that she would bleed in the afternoon. Probably.

She did bleed, as it happened, but she went to the end-of-school-year party anyway. It was not actually the end of the school year since there were lectures scheduled for Monday and Tuesday, and then there were final exams, but it was close enough and everybody needed a party. So Morgan put on a Friday dress and her sweatbands and went.

Jamie O'Hara was tending bar and so Morgan kept away until late in the evening when she had had enough to drink not to care anymore.

"And how is my favorite seminarian?" she said.

"I've missed you," he said. "I've seen you at the parties I've tended, but I guess you didn't see me."

Morgan gave him her ironic smile.

"I guess you did see me and didn't want to."

"Ah," she said.

"Well, how've you been, Morgan?" He said her name in that way of his, and smiled.

Morgan thought for a moment of his cute little buns

and what fun he could be and then she decided in favor of sex.

"I've been mad," she said. "Crazy." She did that thing with her eyes.

"I'll bet," he said, returning the eyes.

"To madness."

As she lifted her drink to toast him, the ruffle at her wrist fell back and Jamie looked from her drink to the white sweatband.

"I see you've still got your stigmata," he said. "It's a great grace."

"Well, I've earned it, don't you think? With my clever hands."

"Your theology is weak, Morgan. You can't earn grace." And as she leaned forward to caress the hair at his wrist, he added, "You can't escape it either."

She pulled her hand away as if she had been stung.

"I'll escape," she said. "You little Catholic bastard."

She went home alone.

•   •   •

Morgan slept all day Saturday and at night, still sick and dizzy from the evening before, she dressed and made up and went off to Gatsby's, a singles bar where the young bachelor types and a few of the more affluent graduate students always hung out. Faculty never went there and so she knew she could pick somebody up in relative privacy. Not that she cared much any longer. Right away she met someone from the business school—a student she had run into once, somewhere—and he bought her a drink. Then she bought him a drink. Already she was drunk. One more drink and she was only partially conscious. The student drove her home, found her key, and lay her on the sofa. She came awake then and, drunken and desperate, grasped his hand. She began to cry softly, still holding on to him. After a long time she stopped. "I can't escape, can I?" she said. "I can't escape." And he, not knowing what to say, wishing only to get away from this crazy woman, agreed with her. "No," he said sadly, "nobody escapes."

· · ·

On Sunday she awoke calm, perfectly composed. She lay on the sofa, still in her dress and heels, and said to the empty room, "I have the stigmata. I am a stigmatic. There is no escape, no place for hiding." She smiled slightly and rolled over and went back to sleep.

Much later in the day she went for a long walk through the campus and thought about what it meant to be who she was. Nothing had changed, she discovered; she was still Morgan Childs, a Ph.D. in mathematics, a mother, a good teacher, a good lover. She could just relax into this new role and, as she had managed everything in her life, she could manage this too. Morgan Childs, Stigmatic.

She had a bottle of wine with dinner, and then poured herself a brandy, and settled down with the telephone.

"Julian?" she said. "How are you, son? How is school?"

"Okay and okay," he said.

"I know," she said. "Julian, you'll be coming home in a couple weeks, Julian, and there's something you should know."

"Uh-oh," he said. "A live-in boyfriend?"

"No, nothing like that. Nothing. It's that I've discovered that, in a way it's impossible to explain, I've become a stigmatic."

"A what?"

"A stigmatic, Juli. It's someone who—"

"You need glasses?"

"Julian, it's somebody who has the wounds of Christ in the hands and feet."

"Oh."

"I only have them in the wrists."

"Ma, are you drinking?"

"Julian. The thing is, they sometimes bleed on Friday."

"That's cool, Ma. I'm on your side."

"It's true, Julian. There's no escape from it."

"You take care, Ma. See you soon."

She held the dead telephone in her hand for a moment and then put it down and picked up her brandy. She would make another attempt. This was, she was certain, the right, the necessary thing to do. She would phone Dr. Underhill, with his watery expertise and his kinky sex games. He answered on the second ring.

"This is Morgan Childs," she said. "Do you remember?"

"Ready for more?" he said.

"Those pains," she said, "in my wrists. Do you remember I saw you about them?"

"What pains?" he said. "What is this?"

"Well, it's the stigmata. I thought you should know."

"When do you want me? I'm ready anytime."

She phoned Jamie O'Hara.

"You were right," she said. "It is the stigmata. And there is no escape."

"Are you all right?" he said. "What's the matter with you?"

"I'm fine," she said. "At last I'm fine."

"You'd better slow down on the booze, lady," Jamie said, but Morgan had already put the receiver down.

She phoned Dr. Sloss, the psychiatrist.

"Some data for you," she said. "That pain was real. It was the stigmata."

"Real pain, imagined pain, it is all one. The question is why you wanted it, why you needed it."

"No, the question is how do you get away from it."

"Is that so? And the answer?"

"There's no getting away from it. There's no escape."

"I've kept your appointment open. You'll want to come back."

"Not now. Not now that I know it's just the stigmata."

"You'll be back. Just try to keep an open mind."

She poured herself another brandy and made one last phone call. She phoned Dr. Aaronson.

"You were right," she said. "It was the stigmata."

"Come and see me, Miss Childs. Let me examine your wrists, yes? We will study this?"

"It's nothing," she said. "I can live with this. I can manage."

•   •   •

On Monday she was to give her last lecture of the school year. She awoke and stretched and thought, Well, I've made it through safely. Nobody knows. Except, of course, the ones she had called, the ones she had had to tell to discharge that obligation. Why had she told them? It had seemed right. Yes, it was right. They had to know. But at once another thought came to her. What if it should happen during the lecture: the pain, the flailing hands, the blood? No, it was Monday. It could not possibly happen on a Monday. Nonetheless, at breakfast she poured a good shot of vodka in her orange juice, just for courage.

By late morning she had become totally preoccupied with the idea that she would suffer an attack during the lecture. She had worn a Friday dress, just in case, and now she put on her sweatbands. She would get through it somehow. She had a small vodka, freshened her lipstick, and walked to the lecture hall.

It was a windup class, pulling everything together and

pointing it all toward the practical, the pragmatic. She had done it often before.

"Everything comes back to facts," she was saying. "There is nothing that cannot be explained once we have a sufficiency of information. The first and final function, then, of a course in statistical analysis is to explain, within a specified field of reference, the likelihood and in some isolated cases the necessity . . ."

And as she had feared, the pain clutched at her wrists and shook her with such violence that the papers flew from her grasp; her hands, flapping, clattered against the lectern. Her head went back and she gave a terrible groan and then pitched forward. Somebody from the first row jumped up and ran to her. She could hear him saying, "Are you all right, Professor Childs? Shall I get somebody? Are you all right?"

Morgan waved him away finally and sat in silence behind the lectern. She was only vaguely aware of the hundred twenty students who sat, silent, motionless, waiting for whatever would happen next. "She's drunk," somebody said. "Or crazy." She heard other comments, remotely; they did not apply to her any longer. She was another person, one none of them knew. Beneath the hot pain she could feel the blood gathering now. It would trickle down her palms, were it not for the sweatbands she had put on. Blood dripping from her wrists to her palms, from her palms to the floor. It would be the ultimate humiliation. Morgan looked out at the faces swimming before her; they were smug, assured; they could explain everything this life would bring them. What they needed was their own assault by the stigmata. And then she thought, I can save them from themselves, I can give them mine. And at once it was clear to her why she had made those phone calls the previous night, why the blood had begun to flow in the middle of her lecture. She would be a witness.

"I must explain," she said, and returned to the podium. "We presume, perhaps rightly, that anything can be explained once we have all the facts. But of course there remains a mystery to fact, to some facts. Take, for example, the fact of the stigmata."

She clutched her hands to her chest as she was assaulted by another wave of pain. When she went on, students had begun to whisper to one another, to shift uneasily in their seats.

"By the stigmata I refer of course to that phenomenon in which certain people throughout history have borne upon their hands and feet, and sometimes in the left side, the wounds of Christ upon the cross. It is a fact that these wounds appear without warning and disappear sometimes without a trace. They bleed real blood, they are extraordinarily painful, they are often accompanied by a kind of ecstasy. It is important to note about the stigmata this further fact: it can happen to anyone, a believer or a nonbeliever. No spiritual or mental or physical superiority is implied. The stigmata is a fact, an assault by the mystery of fact . . . which some call God."

Morgan paused and then turned back the long cuffs of her sleeves and held out her arms to them. "I myself am a stigmatic," she said, and they could see that on each wrist she wore a sweatband, a three-inch absorbent bandage. "Look," she said, and in a final gesture of self-sacrifice, she tore the sweatband from her right wrist and then from her left. "See," she said, extending her wrists to them, her face turned away, her eyes closed. Let them stare at the blood, let them stare at the possibilities ahead of them.

There was silence in the room, and then after a while some whispering, and then she opened her eyes and looked. The sweatbands shone glistening white and her wrists, turned out and displayed for the students, were smooth and unmarked. And yet the pain continued to burn there like some unearthly fire.

• • •

Morgan did not attend graduation. She received many letters of condolence, get-well cards, even bouquets of flowers. The word of her nervous breakdown swept through the campus: delusions of grandeur, religious fanaticism, advanced alcoholism. A major collapse. She was the talk of the university, for over two weeks.

By the beginning of fall semester, however, her collapse seemed nearly forgotten. Morgan was back from a summer's rest in Italy, she had lost a great deal of weight, she looked a little thin but sexy still. So perhaps it had been a minor collapse after all. Everything gets exaggerated in academe.

And yet there was something decidedly different about her. She was ironic now in everything she said, she was teaching less well, she continued to lose weight. But there was something else; she seemed only partly there. In a month or so Morgan was in the hospital with trouble that looked like leukemia but wasn't.

Old Dr. Aaronson came to visit her and was shocked by what he saw. Morgan was hooked up to a number of tubes that fed her and drained her and fortified her blood; but what shocked him was her face. She looked dead. The skin was pulled tight across the bones and her eyes rested in their hollows as if they had been set in stone. When she smiled at him, her lips were thin and bloodless.

"The stigmata?" he said.

"A disease of the blood."

"You still bleed? You still have the wounds? Yes?"

"Not since that time in class." She turned her wrists

toward him; they were smooth and white, with only a tiny white mark on each; an ancient scar or even a skin discoloration, that was all. But no stigmata.

"You should have let me study," he said. "We have missed our one great opportunity. Yes?"

Morgan smiled. "There is no escape," she said.

•   •   •

She died a week later, on a Friday. Her son Julian was there, and so was Jamie O'Hara and Dr. Aaronson. Morgan had been unconscious for some time and the three men were standing by her bedside talking about the weather and then the world series.

Suddenly Morgan was sitting up. Her eyes were open, staring at something above and in front of her. "Oh," she said, and again, with a kind of longing in her voice, "Oh."

And then her hands flew from her sides, shaking furiously, and her whole body convulsed, pulling the tubes from her arms and toppling the I.V. unit. The glass shattered as it hit the floor and a nurse came running in, but nobody else moved. They watched Morgan, who had fallen back against the pillow now, and was gasping for breath, her back arched and her head turned up as if she were leaning eagerly into a long and smothering embrace.

They watched while she held that position for a full minute and part of another. Finally the tension began to drain from her body, slowly at first, and then more completely until at last she lay motionless, her head to one side on the pillow. The nurse moved forward, her hand on Morgan's wrist, feeling for a pulse. "I can manage now," Morgan said with what seemed to be a smile.

Under *cause of death* they wrote: disease of the blood; and under *other significant conditions* they wrote: none.

THE ANATOMY OF

DESIRE

Because Hanley's skin had been stripped off by the enemy, he could find no one who was willing to be with him for long. The nurses were obligated, of course, to see him now and then, and sometimes the doctor, but certainly not the other patients and certainly not his wife and children. He was raw, he was meat, and he would never be any better. He had a great and natural desire, therefore, to be possessed by someone.

He would walk around on his skinned feet, leaving bloody footprints up and down the corridors, looking for someone to love him.

"You're not supposed to be out here," the nurse said. And she added, somehow making it sound kind, "You untidy the floor, Hanley,"

"I want to be loved by someone," he said. "I'm human too. I'm like you."

But he knew he was not like her. Everybody called her the saint.

.   .   .

"Why couldn't it be you?" he said.

She was swabbing his legs with blood retardant, a new discovery that kept Hanley going. It was one of those miracle medications that just grew out of the war.

"I wasn't chosen," she said. "I have my skin."

"No," he said. "I mean why couldn't it be you who will love me, possess me? I have desires too," he said.

She considered this as she swabbed his shins and the soles of his feet.

"I have no desires," she said. "Or only one. It's the same thing."

He looked at her loving face. It was not a pretty face, but it was saintly.

"Then you will?" he said.

"If I come to know sometime that I must," she said.

.   .   .

The enemy had not chosen Hanley, they had just lucked upon him sleeping in his trench. They were a raid party of four, terrified and obedient, and they had been told to bring back an enemy to serve as an example of what is done to infiltrators.

They dragged Hanley back across the line and ran him, with his hands tied behind his back, the two kilometers to the general's tent.

The general dismissed the guards because he was very taken with Hanley. He untied the cords that bound his wrists and let his arms hang free. Then slowly, ritually, he tipped Hanley's face toward the light and examined it carefully. He kissed him on the brow and on the cheek and finally on the mouth. He gazed deep and long into Hanley's eyes until he saw his own reflection there looking back. He traced the lines of Hanley's eyebrows, gently, with the tip of his index finger. "Such a beautiful face," he said in his own language. He pressed his palms lightly against Hanley's forehead, against his cheekbones, his jaw. With his little finger he memorized the shape of Hanley's lips, the laugh lines at his eyes, the chin. The general did Hanley's face very thoroughly. Afterward he did some things down below, and so just before sunrise when the time came to lead Hanley out to the stripping post, he told the soldiers with the knives: "This young man could be my own son; so spare him here and here."

The stripping post stood dead-center in the line of barbed wire only a few meters beyond the range of gunfire. A loudspeaker was set up and began to blare the day's message. "This is what happens to infiltrators. No infiltrators will be spared." And then as troops from both sides watched through binoculars, the enemy cut the skin from Hanley's body, sparing—as the general had insisted—his face and his genitals. They were skilled men and the skin was stripped off expeditiously and they hung it, headless, on the barbed wire as an example. They lay Hanley himself on the ground where he could die.

He was rescued a little after noon when the enemy, for no good reason, went into sudden retreat.

Hanley was given emergency treatment at the field unit, and when they had done what they could for him, they sent him on to the vets' hospital. At least there, they told each other, he will be attended by the saint.

·   ·   ·

It was quite some time before the saint said yes, she would love him.

"Not just love me. Possess me."

"There are natural reluctancies," she said. "There are personal peculiarities," she said. "You will have to have patience with me."

"You're supposed to be a saint," he said.

So she lay down with him in his bloody bed and he found great satisfaction in holding this small woman in his arms. He kissed her and caressed her and felt young and whole again. He did not miss his wife and children. He did not miss his skin.

The saint did everything she must. She told him how handsome he was and what pleasure he gave her. She touched him in the way he liked best. She said he was her whole life, her fate. And at night when he woke her to staunch the blood, she whispered how she needed him, how she could not live without him.

This went on for some time.

.   .   .

The war was over and the occupying forces had made the general mayor of the capital city. He was about to run for senator and wanted his past to be beyond the reproach of any investigative committee. He wrote Hanley a letter which he sent through the International Red Cross.

"You could have been my own son," he said. "What we do in war is what we have to do. We do not choose cruelty or violence. I did only what was my duty."

.   .   .

"I am in love and I am loved," Hanley said. "Why isn't this enough?"

The saint was swabbing his chest and belly with blood retardant.

"Nothing is ever enough," she said.

"I love, but I am not possessed by love," he said. "I want to be surrounded by you. I want to be enclosed. I want to be enveloped. I don't have the words for it. But do you understand?"

"You want to be possessed," she said.

"I want to be inside you."

And so they made love, but afterward he said, "That is not enough. That is only a metaphor for what I want."

     •   •   •

The general was elected senator and was made a trustee of three nuclear-arms conglomerates. But he was not well. And he was not sleeping well.

He wrote to Hanley, "I wake in the night and see your face before mine. I feel your forehead pressing against my palms. I taste your breath. I did only what I had to do. You could have been my son."

     •   •   •

"I know what I want," Hanley said.

"If I can do it, I will," the saint said.

"I want your skin."

And so she lay down on the long white table, shuddering, while Hanley made his first incision. He cut along the shoulders and then down the arms and back up, then down the sides and the legs to the feet. It took him longer than he had expected. The saint shivered at the cold touch of the knife and she sobbed once at the sight of the blood, but by the time Hanley lifted the shroud of skin from her crimson body, she was resigned, satisfied even.

Hanley had spared her face and her genitals.

He spread the skin out to dry and, while he waited, he swabbed her raw body carefully with blood retardant. He whispered little words of love and thanks and desire to her.

A smile played about her lips but she said nothing.

It would be a week before he could put on her skin.

•   •   •

The general wrote to Hanley one last letter. "I can endure no more. I am possessed by you."

•   •   •

Hanley put on the skin of the saint. His genitals fitted nicely through the gap he had left and the skin at his neck matched hers exactly. He walked the corridors and for once left no bloody tracks behind. He stood before mirrors and admired himself. He touched his breasts and his belly and his thighs and there was no blood on his hands.

"Thank you," he said to her. "It is my heart's desire fulfilled. I am inside you. I am possessed by you."

And then, in the night, he kissed her on the brow and on the cheek and finally on the mouth. He gazed deep and long into her eyes. He traced the lines of her eyebrows gently, with the tip of his index finger. "Such a beautiful face," he said. He pressed his palms lightly against her forehead, her cheekbones, her jaw. With his little finger he memorized the shape of her lips.

And then it was that Hanley, loved, desperate to possess and be possessed, staring deep into the green and loving eyes of the saint, saw that there can be no possession, there is only desire. He plucked at his empty skin, and wept.

FOR THE BEST IN PAPERBACKS, LOOK FOR THE

In every corner of the world, on every subject under the sun, Penguin represents quality and variety—the very best in publishing today.

For complete information about books available from Penguin—including Pelicans, Puffins, Peregrines, and Penguin Classics—and how to order them, write to us at the appropriate address below. Please note that for copyright reasons the selection of books varies from country to country.

In the United Kingdom: For a complete list of books available from Penguin in the U.K., please write to *Dept E.P., Penguin Books Ltd, Harmondsworth, Middlesex, UB7 0DA.*

In the United States: For a complete list of books available from Penguin in the U.S., please write to *Dept BA, Penguin*, Box 120, Bergenfield, New Jersey 07621-0120.

In Canada: For a complete list of books available from Penguin in Canada, please write to *Penguin Books Canada Ltd, 10 Alcorn Avenue, Suite 300, Toronto, Ontario, Canada M4V 3B2.*

In Australia: For a complete list of books available from Penguin in Australia, please write to the *Marketing Department, Penguin Books Ltd, P.O. Box 257, Ringwood, Victoria 3134.*

In New Zealand: For a complete list of books available from Penguin in New Zealand, please write to the *Marketing Department, Penguin Books (NZ) Ltd, Private Bag, Takapuna, Auckland 9.*

In India: For a complete list of books available from Penguin, please write to *Penguin Overseas Ltd, 706 Eros Apartments, 56 Nehru Place, New Delhi, 110019.*

In Holland: For a complete list of books available from Penguin in Holland, please write to *Penguin Books Nederland B.V., Postbus 195, NL-1380AD Weesp, Netherlands.*

In Germany: For a complete list of books available from Penguin, please write to *Penguin Books Ltd, Friedrichstrasse 10-12, D-6000 Frankfurt Main 1, Federal Republic of Germany.*

In Spain: For a complete list of books available from Penguin in Spain, please write to *Longman, Penguin España, Calle San Nicolas 15, E-28013 Madrid, Spain.*

In Japan: For a complete list of books available from Penguin in Japan, please write to *Longman Penguin Japan Co Ltd, Yamaguchi Building, 2-12-9 Kanda Jimbocho, Chiyoda-Ku, Tokyo 101, Japan.*